The Avalanche

Gertrude Franklin Horn Atherton

Contents

THE AVALANCHE

BY

Gertrude Franklin Horn Atherton

TO CHARLES HANSON TOWNE

CHAPTER I

I

Price Ruyler knew that many secrets had been inhumed by the earthquake and fire of San Francisco and wondered if his wife's had been one of them. After all, she had been born in this city of odd and whispered pasts, and there were moments when his silent mother-in-law suggested a past of her own.

That there was a secret of some sort he had been progressively convinced for quite six months. Moreover, he felt equally sure that this impalpable gray cloud had not drifted even transiently between himself and his wife during the first year and a half of their marriage. They had been uncommonly happy; they were happy yet ... the difference lay not in the quality of Helene's devotion, enhanced always by an outspoken admiration for himself and his achievements, but in subtle changes of temperament and spirits.

She had been a gay and irresponsible young creature when he married her, so much so that he had found it expedient to put her on an allowance and ask her not to ran up staggering bills in the fashionable shops; which she visited daily, as much for the pleasure of the informal encounter with other lively and irresponsible young luminaries of San Francisco society as for the excitement of buying what she did not want.

He had broached the subject with some trepidation, for they had never had a quarrel; but she had shown no resentment whatever, merely an eager desire to please him. She even went directly down to the Palace Hotel and reproached her august parent for failing to warn her that a dollar was not capable of infinite expansion.

But no wonder she had been extravagant, she told Ruyler plaintively. It had been like a fairy tale, this sudden release from the rigid economies of her girlhood, when she had rarely had a franc in her pocket, and they had lived in a suite of the old family villa on one of the hills of Rouen, Madame Delano paying her brother for their lodging, and dressing herself and Helene with the aid of a half paralyzed seamstress with a fiery red nose. Ma foi! It was the nightmare of her youth, that nose and that croaking voice. But the woman had fingers, and a taste! And her mother could have concocted a smart evening frock out of an old window curtain.

But the petted little daughter was never asked to go out and buy a spool of thread, much less was she consulted in the household economies. All she noticed was that her clothes were smarter than Cousin Marthe's, who had a real dressmaker, and was subject to fits of jealous sulks. No wonder that when money was poured into her lap out in this wonderful California she had assumed that it was made only to spend.

But she would learn! She would learn! She would ask her mother that very day to initiate her into the fascinating secrets of personal economies, teach her how to portion out her quarterly allowance between her wardrobe, club dues, charities, even her private automobile.

This last heroic suggestion was her own, and although her husband protested he finally agreed; it was well she should learn just what it cost to be a woman of fashion in San Francisco, and the allowance was very generous. His old steward, Mannings, ran the household, although as he went through the form of laying the bills before his little mistress on the third of every month, she knew that the upkeep of the San Francisco house and the Burlingame villa ran into a small fortune a year.

"It is not that I am threatened with financial disaster," Ruyler had said to her. "But San Francisco has not recovered yet, and it is impossible to say just when she will recover. I want to be absolutely sure of my expenditures."

She had promised vehemently, and, as far as he knew, she had kept her promise. He had received no more bills, and it was obvious that her haughty chauffeur was paid on schedule time, until, seized with another economical spasm, she sold her car and bought a small electric which she could drive herself.

Ruyler, little as he liked his mother-in-law, was intensely grateful to her for the dexterity with which she had adjusted Helene's mind to the new condition. She even taught her how to keep books in an elemental way and balanced them herself on the first of every month. As Helene Ruyler had a mind as quick and supple as it was cultivated in *les graces*, she soon ceased to feel the chafing of her new harness, although she did squander the sum she had reserved for three months mere pocket money upon a hat; which was sent to the house by her wily milliner on the first day of the second quarter. She confessed this with tears, and her husband, who thought her feminine passion for hats adorable, dried her tears and took her to the opening night of a new play. But he did not furnish the pathetic little gold mesh bag, and as he made her promise not to borrow, she did not treat her friends to tea or ices at any of the fashionable rendezvous for a month. Then her native French thrift came to her aid and she sold a superfluous gold purse, a wedding present, to an envious friend at a handsome bargain.

That was ancient history now. It was twenty months since Price had received a bill, and secret inquiries during the past two had satisfied him that his wife's name was written in the books of no shop in San Francisco that she would condescend to visit. Therefore, this maddening but intangible barrier had nothing to do with a change of habit that had not caused an hour of tears and sulks. Helene had a quick temper but a gay and sweet disposition, normally high spirits, little apparent selfishness, and a naive adoration of masculine superiority and strength; altogether, with her high bred beauty and her dignity in public, an enchanting creature and an ideal wife for a busy man of inherited social position and no small degree of pride.

But all this lovely equipment was blurred, almost obscured at times, by the shadow that he was beginning to liken to the San Francisco fogs that drifted through the Golden Gate and settled down into the deep hollows of the Marin hills; moving gently but restlessly even there, like ghostly floating tides. He could see them from his library window, where he often finished his afternoon's work with his secretaries.

But the fog drifted back to the Pacific, and the shadow that encompassed his wife did not, or rarely. It chilled their ardors, even their serene domesticity. She was often as gay and impulsive as ever, but with abrupt reserves, an implication not only of a new maturity of spirit, but of watchfulness, even fear. She had once gone so far as to give voice passionately to the dogma that no two mortals had the right to be as happy as they were; then laughed apologetically and "guessed" that the old Puritan spirit of her father's people was coming to life in her Gallic little soul; then, with another change of mood, added defiantly that it was time America were rid of its baneful inheritance, and that she would be happy to-day if the skies fell to-morrow. She had flung herself into her husband's arms, and even while he embraced her the eyes of his spirit searched for the girl wife who had fled and left this more subtly fascinating but incomprehensible creature in her place.

II

The morning was Sunday and he sat in the large window of his library that overlooked the Bay of San Francisco. The house, which stood on one of the highest hills, he had bought and remodeled for his bride. The books that lined these walls had belonged to his Ruyler grandfather, bought in a day when business men had time to read and it was the fashion for a gentleman to cultivate the intellectual tracts of his brain. The portraits that hung above, against the dark paneling, were the work of his mother's father, one of the celebrated portrait painters of his time, and were replicas of the eminent and mighty he had painted. Maharajas, kings, emperors, famous diplomats, men of letters, artists of his own small class, statesmen and several of the famous beauties of their brief day; these had been the favorite grandson's inheritance from Masewell Price, and they made an impressive frieze, unique in the splendid homes of the city of Ruyler's adoption.

He had brought them from New York when he had decided to live in California, and hung them in his bachelor quarters. He had soon made up his mind that he must remain in San Francisco for at least ten years if he would maintain the business he had rescued from the disaster of 1906 at the level where he had, by the severest application of his life, placed it by the end of 1908. Meanwhile he had grown to like San Francisco better than he would have believed possible when he arrived in the wrecked city, still smoking, and haunted with the subtle odors of fires that had consumed more than products of the vegetable kingdom.

The vast ruin with its tottering arches and broken columns, its lonely walls looking as if bitten by prehistoric monsters that must haunt this ancient coast, the soft pastel colors the great fire had given as sole compensation for all it had taken, the grotesque twisted masses of steel and the aged gray hills that had looked down on so many fires, had appealed powerfully to his imagination, and made him feel, when wandering alone at night, as if his brain cells were haunted by old memories of Antioch when Nature had annihilated in an instant what man had lavished upon her for centuries. Nowhere, not even in what was left of ancient Rome, had he ever received such an impression of the age of the world and of the nothingness of man as among the ruins of this ridiculously modern city of San Francisco. It fascinated him, but he told himself then that he should leave it without a pang. He was a New Yorker of the seventh generation of his house, and the rest of the United States of America was merely incidental.

The business, a branch of the great New York firm founded in 1840 by an ancestor grown weary of watching the broad acres of Ruyler Manor automatically transmute themselves into the yearly rent-roll, and reverting to the energy and merchant instincts of his Dutch ancestors, had been conducted skillfully for the thirty years preceding the disaster by Price's uncle, Dryden Ruyler. But the earthquake and fire in which so many uninsured millions had vanished, had also wrecked men past the rebounding age, and Dryden Ruyler was one of them. He might have borne the destruction of the old business building down on Front Street, or even the temporary stagnation of trade, but when the Pacific Union Club disappeared in the raging furnace, and, like many of his old cronies who had no home either in the country or out in the Western Addition, he was driven over to Oakland for lodgings, this ghastly climax of horrors--he escaped in a milk wagon after sleeping for two nights without shelter on the bare hills behind San Francisco, while the fire roared its defiance to the futile detonations of dynamite, and his sciatica was as fiery as the atmosphere--had broken the old man's spirit, and he had announced his determination to return to Ruyler-on-Hudson and die as a gentleman should.

There was no question of Price's father, Morgan Ruyler, leaving New York, even if he had contemplated the sacrifice for a moment; that his second son and general manager of the several branches of the great business of Ruyler and Sons--as integral a part of the ancient history of San Francisco as of the comparatively modern history of New York--should go, was so much a matter of course that Price had taken the first Overland train that left New York after the receipt of his uncle's despairing telegram.

In spite of the fortune behind him and his own expert training, the struggle to rebuild the old business to its former standard had been unintermittent. The terrific shock to the city's energies was followed by a general depression, and the insane spending of a certain class of San Franciscans when their insurance money was paid, was like a brief last crackling in a cold stove, and, moreover, was of no help to the wholesale houses.

But Price Ruyler, like so many of his new associates in like case, had emerged triumphant; and with the unqualified approval and respect of the substantial citizens of San Francisco.

It was this position he had won in a community where he had experienced the unique sensation of being a pioneer in at the rebirth of a great city, as well as the outdoor sports that kept him fit, that had endeared California to Ruyler, and in time caused him whimsically to visualize New York as a sternly accusing instead of a beckoning finger. Long before he found time to play polo at Burlingame he had conceived a deep respect for a climate where a man might ride horseback, shoot, drive a racing car, or tramp, for at least eight months of the year with no menace of sudden downpour, and hardly a change in the weight of his clothes.

To-day the rain was dashing against his windows and the wind howled about the exposed angles of his house with that personal fury of assault with which storms brewed out in the vast wastes of the Pacific deride the enthusiastic baptism of a too confident explorer. All he could see of the bay was a mad race of white caps, and dark blurs which only memory assured him were rocky storm-beaten islands; mountain tops, so geological tradition ran, whose roots were in an unquiet valley long since dropped from mortal gaze.

The waves were leaping high against the old forts at the entrance to the Golden Gate, and occasionally he saw a small craft drift perilously near to the rocks. But he loved the wild weather of San Francisco, for he was by nature an imaginative man and he liked to think that he would have followed the career of letters had not the traditions of the great commercial house of Ruyler and Sons, forced him to carry on the burden.

The men of his family had never been idlers since the recrudescence of ancestral energy in the person of Morgan Ruyler I; it was no part of their profound sense of aristocracy to retire on inherited or invested wealth; they believed that your fine American of the old stock should die in harness; and if the harness had been fashioned and elaborated by ancestors whose portraits hung in the Chamber of Commerce, all the more reason to keep it spic and up to date instead of letting it lapse into those historic vaults where so many once honored names lay rotting. They were a hard, tight-fisted lot, the Ruylers, and Price in one secluded but cherished wing of his mind was unlike them only because his mother was the daughter of Masefield Price and would have been an artist herself if her scandalized husband would have consented. Morgan Ruyler IV had overlooked his father-in-law's divagation from the orthodox standards of his own family because he had been a spectacular financial success; bringing home ropes of enormous pearls from India in addition to the fantastic sums paid him by enraptured native princes. But while Morgan Ruyler believed that rich men should work and make their sons work, if only because an idle class was both out of place in a republic and conducive to unrest in the masses, it was quite otherwise with women. They were for men to shelter, and it was their sole duty to be useful in the home, and, wherever possible, ornamental in public. Nor had he the least faith in female talent.

Marian Ruyler had yielded the point and departed hopefully for a broader sphere when her second and favorite son was eight. Morgan Ruyler married again as soon as convention would permit, this time carefully selecting a wife of the soundest New York predispositions and with a personal admiration of Queen Victoria; and he had watched young Price like an affectionate but inexorable parent hawk until the young man followed his brother--a quintessential Ruyler--into the now historic firm. However, he suffered little from anxiety. Price, too, was conservative, intensely proud of the family traditions, an almost impassioned worker, and unselfish as men go. Two sons in every generation must enter the firm. It was not in the Ruyler blood to take long chances.

III

Life out here in California had been too hurried for more than fleeting moments of self-study, but on this idle Sunday morning Price Ruyler's perturbed mind wandered to that inner self of his to which he once had longed to give a freer expression. It was odd that the conservative training, the rigid traditions of his family, conventional, old-fashioned, Puritanical, as became the best stock of New York, a stock that in the Ruyler family had seemed to carry its own antidote for the poisons ever seeking entrance to the spiritual conduits of the rich, had left any place for that sentimental romantic tide in his nature which had swept him into marriage with a girl outside of his own class; a girl of whose family he had known practically nothing until his outraged father had cabled to a correspondent in Paris to make investigation of the Perrin family of Rouen, to which the girl's mother claimed to belong.

The inquiries were satisfactory; they were quite respectable, bourgeois, silk merchants in a small way--although at least two strata below that haute bourgeoisie which now regarded itself as the real upper class of the Republique Francaise. A true Ruyler, however, would have fled at the first danger signal, never have reached the point where inquiries were in order.

California was replete with charming, beautiful, and superlatively healthy girls; the climate produced them as it did its superabundance of fruit, flowers, and vegetables. But they had left Price Ruyler untroubled. He had been far more interested watching San Francisco rise from its ruins, transformed almost overnight from a picturesque but ramshackle city, a patchwork of different eras, into a staid metropolis of concrete and steel, defiant alike of earthquake and fire. He had liked the new experience of being a pioneer, which so subtly expanded his starved ego that he had, by unconscious degrees, made up his mind to remain out here as the permanent head of the San Francisco House; and in time, no doubt, marry one of these fine, hardy, frank, out-of-door, wholly unsubtle California girls. Moreover, he had found in San Francisco several New Yorkers as well as Englishmen of his own class--notably John Gwynne, who had thrown over one of the greatest of English peerages to follow his personal tastes in a legislative career--all of whom had settled down into that free and independent life from motives not dissimilar from his own.

But he had ceased to be an untroubled spirit from the moment he met Helene Delano. He had gone down to Monterey for polo, and he had forgotten the dinner to which he had brought a keen appetite, and stared at her as she entered the immense dining room with her mother.

It was not her beauty, although that was considerable, that had summarily transposed his gallant if cool admiration for all charming well bred women into a submerging recognition of woman in particular; it was her unlikeness to any of the girls he had been riding, dancing, playing golf and tennis with during the past year and a half (for two years after his arrival he had seen nothing of society whatever). Later that evening he defined this dissimilarity from the American girl as the result not only of her French blood but of her European training, her quiet secluded girl-hood in a provincial town of great beauty, where she had received a leisurely education rare in the United States, seen or read little of the great world (she had visited Paris only twice and briefly), her mind charmingly developed by conscientious tutors. But at the moment he thought that the compelling power lay in some deep subtlety of eye, her little air of lofty aloofness, her classic small features in a small face, and the top-heavy masses of blue black hair which she carried with a certain naive pride as if it were her only vanity; in her general unlikeness to the gray-eyed fair-haired American--a type to which himself belonged. Her only point in common with this fashionable set patronizing Del Monte for the hour, was the ineffable style with which she wore her perfect little white frock; an American inheritance, he assumed after he knew her; for, as he recalled provincial French women, style was not their strong point.

When he met her eyes some twenty minutes later, he dismissed the impression of subtlety, for their black depths were quick with an eager wonder and curiosity. Later they grew wistful, and he guessed that she knew none of these smart folk, down, like himself, for the tournament; people who were chattering from table to table like a large family. That some of his girl acquaintances were interested in the young stranger he inferred from speculative and appraising eyes that were turned upon her from time to time.

Price, with some irony, wondered at their curiosity. The San Francisco girl, he had discovered, possessed an extra sense all her own. There was no lofty indifference about her. She had the worth-while stranger detected and tabulated and his or her social destiny settled before the Eastern train had disgorged its contents at the Oakland mole. And even the immense florid mother of this lovely girl, with her own masses of snow white hair dressed in a manner becoming her age, and a severe gown of black Chantilly net, relieved by the merest trifle of jet, looked the reverse of the nondescript tourist. The girl wore white embroidered silk muslin and a thin gold chain with a small ruby pendant. She was rather above the average height, although not as tall as her mother, and if she were as thin as fashion commanded, her bones were so small that her neck and arms looked almost plump. Her expressive eyes were as black as her hair, and her only large feature. Her skin was of a quite remarkably pink whiteness, although there was a pink color in her lips and cheeks. The older men stared at her more persistently than the younger ones, who liked their own sort and not girls who looked as if they might be "booky" and "spring things on a fellow."

There was a ball in the evening and once more mother and daughter sat apart, while the flower of San Francisco--an inclusive term for the select circles of Menlo Park, Atherton, Burlingame, San Mateo, far San Rafael and Belvedere--romped as one great family. Newport, Ruyler reflected for the twentieth time, did it no better. To the stranger peering through the magic bars they were now as insensible as befitted their code. These two people knew nobody and that was the end of it.

IV

But Price noted that now the girl's eyes were merely wistful, and once or twice he saw them fill with tears. As three of the dowagers merely sniffed when he sought possible information, he finally had recourse to the manager of the hotel, D.V. Bimmer. They were a Madame and Mademoiselle Delano from Rouen, and had been at the hotel for a fortnight, not seeming to mind its comparative emptiness, but enjoying the sea bathing and the drives. The girl rode, and went out every morning with a groom.

"But didn't they bring any letters?" asked Ruyler. "They are ladies and one letter would have done the business. That poor girl is having the deuce of a time."

"D.V.," who knew "everybody" in California, and all their secrets, shook his head. "'Fraid not. The French maid told the floor valet that although the father was American--from New England somewheres--and the girl born in California, accidentally as it were, she had lived in France all her life--she's just eighteen--never crossed the ocean before. Can you beat it? Until last month, and then they came from Hong Kong--taking a trip round the world in good old style. The madame, who scarcely opens her month, did condescend to tell me that she had admired California very much when she was here before, and intended to travel all over the state. Perhaps I met her in that far off long ago, for I was managing a hotel in San Francisco about that time, and her face haunts me somehow--although when features get all swallowed up by fat like that you can't locate them. The girl, too, reminds me of some one, but of course she was in arms when she left and as I ain't much on cathedrals I never went to Rouen. Of course it's the old trick, bringing a pretty girl to a fashionable watering place to marry her off, but these folks are not poor. Not what we'd call rich, perhaps, but good and solid. I don't fall for the old lady; she's a cool proposition or I miss my guess, but the girl's all right. I've seen too many girls in this Mecca for adventurous females and never made a mistake yet. I wish some of our grand dames would extend the glad hand. But I'm afraid they won't. Terrible exclusive, this bunch."

Ruyler scowled and walked back to the ballroom. The exclusiveness of this young society on the wrong side of the continent sometimes made him homesick and sometimes made him sick. He saw little chance for this poor girl to enjoy the rights of her radiant youth if her mother had not taken the precaution to bring letters. France was full of Californians. Many lived there. Surely she must have met some one she could have made use of. It was tragic to watch a pathetic young thing staring at two or three hundred young men and maidens disporting themselves with the natural hilarity of youth, and but few of them too ill-natured to welcome a young and lovely stranger if properly introduced.

He experienced a desperate impulse to go up to the mother and offer her the hospitality of the evening, ask her to regard him as her host. But Madame Delano had a frozen eye, and no doubt orthodox French ideas on the subject of young girls.

A moment later his eye fell on Mrs. Ford Thornton.

"Fordy" was many times a millionaire, and his handsome intelligent wife lived the life of her class. But she was far less conservative than any woman Price had met in San Francisco. Although she was no longer young he had more than once detected symptoms of a wild and insurgent spirit, and an impatient contempt for the routine she was compelled to follow or go into retirement. She was always leaving abruptly for Europe, and every once in a while she did something quite uncanonical; enjoying wickedly the consternation she caused among the serenely regulated, and betraying to the keen eyes of the New Yorker an ironic appreciation of the immense wealth which enabled her to do as she chose, answerable to no one. Her husband was uxorious and she had no children. She had seemed to Price more restless than usual of late and showing unmistakable signs of abrupt departure. (He was sure she dusted the soles of her boots as she locked the door of drawing-room A.) Perhaps to-night she might be in a schismatic mood.

She was standing apart, a tall, dark, almost fiercely haughty woman, but dressed with a certain arrogant simplicity, without jewels, her hair in a careless knot at the base of her head. There were times when she was impeccably groomed, others when she looked as if an infuriated maid had left her helpless. She was, as Ruyler well knew, a kind and generous woman (in certain of her moods), with whom the dastardly cradle fates had experimented, hoping for high drama when the whip of life snapped once too often. Perhaps she had found her revenge as well as her consolation in cheating them.

It was evident to Price that she had been snubbing somebody, for a group of matrons, flushed and drawn apart, were whispering resentfully. Price Ruyler stood in no awe of her. He could match her arrogance, and he liked and admired her more than any of his new friends. They quarreled furiously but she had never snubbed him.

He walked over to her, his cool gray eyes lit with the pleasure in seeing her that she had learned to expect. "Good evening, oh, Queen of the Pacific," he said lightly. "You are looking quite wonderful as usual. Are you standing alone almost in the middle of the room to emphasize the--difference?"

"I am in no mood for compliments, satiric or otherwise." She looked him over with cool penetration. "I may not massage or have my old cuticle ripped off. If I

choose to look my age you must admit that it gives me one more claim to original-
ity."

"You should have let the world know long since just how original you are, instead of settling down into the leadership of San Francisco society--"

He enjoyed provoking her. Her dark narrow eyes opened and flashed as they
must have done in their unchastened youth. "Don't dare call me the leader of this-
-this!"

"Granted. But the fact remains that your word alone is law. Therefore I am
about to ask you to forget that I am a bungling diplomat and do a kind act. For once
you would be able to be both kind and original."

"I did not know you went in for charities. I am sick of shelling out."

"My only part in charities is shelling out."

"Well, come to the point. What do you want?"

"I want you to go over to that lady--Madame Delano, her name is--sitting beside that beautiful girl, and introduce yourself and then me. They are strangers and
I'd like to give them a good time."

"How disinterested of you!" She looked the isolated couple over. "The girl is all
right, but I don't like the mother. She is well dressed--oh, correct from tip to toe--
but not quite the lady."

Ruyler's cool insolent gaze swept the dado of amiable overfed ladies who fanned
themselves against the wall.

"None of that! You know that I do not tolerate the New York attitude. At
least we know who ours are; they came into their own respectably, and with no
uncertain touch. Of course it is stupid of them to get fat. Naturally it makes them
look *bourgeoise*. But this is a lazy climate. As to that woman: there is something
about her I do not like. She is aggressively not massaged, not made up. Only a
woman of assured position can afford to be mid-Victorian. It is now quite the smart
thing to make up."

"No doubt her position is assured in her own provincial town. It will be easy
enough to drop her if she doesn't go down. You can't deny that the girl is all right-
-and a sweet pathetic figure."

"If the girl marries one of our boys--and no doubt that is what she was brought
here for--we shall not be able to get rid of the mother. We've tried that and

failed."

At that moment Ruyler's eyes met those of the girl. They flashed an irresistible appeal. He drew a short breath. How different she looked! She radiated a subtle promise of perfect companionship. Price Ruyler did what all men will do until the end of time. He made up his mind that he had found his woman and without vocal assistance.

Mrs. Thornton, who had been watching the unusual mobility of his face, met his eyes with a satirical smile in her own, her thin red curling lips drawn almost straight for a moment. She had played with the fancy, before anger banished it, that if she had been twenty years younger.... Men had fallen madly in love with her in her own day.... She detected the symptoms in this man at once. Her savage will compelled her to accept accumulating years without a concession. But she had forgotten nothing.

Ruyler may have read her thoughts.

"You know," he said, with an attempt at lightness, although the coast wind tan, which was his only claim to coloring, had paled a little, "that girl reminds me so much of you that I have made up my mind to marry her. I don't care who she is. If you don't help me to meet her conventionally I'll manage somehow, but I should hate to practice any subterfuges on the woman I intend to make my wife."

For a moment he had the sensation of being pinned to the wall by that narrow concentrated gaze. Then Mrs. Thornton swung on her heel. "I'll do it," she said.

She walked across the room with the supple grace her slender figure had never lost and sat down beside the older woman. In a moment the astonished dowagers who had "suffered from her fiendish temper all evening," saw her talking with spontaneous graciousness to both the strangers. Madame Delano was at first more distant and reserved than Mrs. Thornton had ever been, manifestly betraying all the suspicion and unsocial instincts of her class; but she thawed, and the two women chatted, while once more the girl's eyes wandered to the dancers.

When Mrs. Thornton had tormented Ruyler for quite fifteen minutes she beckoned to him imperiously. A moment later he was whirling the girl down the ball room and thrilling at her contact.

V

The wooing had been as headlong as his falling in love. Helene Delano had a deep sweet voice, which completed the conquest during the hour they spent in the grounds under the shelter of a great palm, until hunted down by a horrified parent.

Helene talked frankly of her life. Her mother had been visiting relatives in a small New England town--Holbrook Centre, she believed it was called, but hard American names did not cling to her memory--she loved the soft Latin and Indian names in California--and there she had met and married her father, James Delano. They were on their way to Japan when business detained him in San Francisco much longer than he had expected and she was born. She believed that he had owned a ranch that he wanted to sell. He died on the voyage across the Pacific and her mother had returned to live among her own people in Rouen--very plain bourgeois, but of a respectability, Oh, la! la!

"But it was a tiresome life for a young girl with American blood in her, monsieur." Her mother's income from her husband's estate was not large, but they lived in a wing of the old house and were very comfortable. From her window there was a lovely view of the Seine winding off to Paris. "Oh, monsieur, how I used to long to go to Paris! America was too far. I never even dreamed of it. But Paris! And only two little glimpses of it--the last when we spent a fortnight there before sailing, to get me some nice frocks...."

She had studied hard--but hard! She knew four languages, she told Ruyler proudly. "I had no *dot* then, you see. It was possible I might have to teach one day. A governess in England, Oh, la! la!"

But six months ago a good old uncle had died and left them some money. She would have a little *dot* now, and they could travel. Maman said she would not have a large enough *dot* to make a fine marriage in France, but that the English and American men were more romantic. They went first to the Orient, as there were many Englishmen of good family to be met there. "But maman is difficult to please," she added with her enchanting artlessness, "as difficult as I myself, monsieur. I wish to fall in love like the American girls. Maman says it is not necessary, but I am half American, so, why not? There was an English gentleman with a nice title in Hong Kong and maman was quite pleased with him until she discovered that he gambled or did something equally horrid and she bought our tickets for San Francisco right away."

Yes, she was enjoying her travels, but she was a little lonesome; in Rouen at least she had her cousins. For the first time in her life she was talking to a young man alone; even on the steamer she was not permitted to speak to any of the nice young men who looked as if they would like her if only maman would relent.

"In our ugly old rooms in Rouen maman cherished me like some rare little flower in an old earthen pot," she added quaintly. "Now the pot has tinsel and tissue paper round it, but until to-night I have felt as if I might just as well be an old cabbage."

But it had been heaven to dance with a young man who was not a cousin; and to sit out alone with him in the moonlight, Oh, **grace a Dieu**!

Traveling she had read modern novels for the first time. There were many in the ship's library, oh, but dozens! and she knew now how American and English girls enjoyed life. Her mother had been ill nearly all the way over. She had given her word not to speak to any one, but maman had been ignorant of the library replete with the novelists of the day, and although she was not untruthful, **enfin**, she saw no reason to ask her too anxious parent for another prohibition and condemn herself to yawn at the sea.

Ruyler proposed at the end of a week. She was the only really innocent, unspoiled, unselfconscious girl he had ever met, almost as old-fashioned as his great grandmother must have been. Not that he set forth her virtues to bolster his determination to marry a girl of no family even in her own country; he was madly in love, and life without her was unthinkable; but he tabulated the thousand points to her credit for the benefit of his outraged father.

He did not pretend to like Madame Delano. She was a hard, calculating, sordid old bourgeoisie, but when he refused the little **dot** she would have settled upon Helene, he knew that he had won her friendship and that she would give him no trouble. She was not a mother-in-law to be ashamed of, for her manners were coldly correct, her education in youth had evidently been adequate, and in her obese way she was imposing. She gave him to understand that she had no more desire to live with her son-in-law than he with her, and established herself in a small suite in the Palace Hotel. After a "lifetime" in a provincial town, economizing mercilessly, she felt, she remarked in one of her rare expansive moments, that she had earned the right to look on at life in a great hotel.

The rainy season she spent in Southern California, moving from one large hotel crowded with Eastern visitors to another. This uncommon self-indulgence and her devotion to Helene were the only weak spots Ruyler was able to discover in that cast-iron character. She seldom attended the brilliant entertainments of her daughter and refused the endowed car offered by her son-in-law. Helene married to the best *parti* in San Francisco and quite happy, she seemed content to settle down into the role of the onlooker at the kaleidoscope of life. She spent eight hours of the day and evening seated in an arm chair in the court of the Palace Hotel, and for air rode out to the end of the California Street car line, always on the front seat of the dummy. She was dubbed a "quaint old party" by her new acquaintances and left to her own devices. If she didn't want them they could jolly well do without her.

VI

Helene's social success was immediate and permanent. Californians rarely do things by halves. Society was no exception. She had "walked off" with the most desirable man in town, but they were good gamblers. When they lost they paid. She had married into "their set." They had accepted her. She was one of them. No secret order is more loyal to its initiates.

During that first year and a half of ideal happiness Ruyler, in what leisure he could command, found Helene's rapidly expanding mind as companionable as he had hoped; and the girlish dignity she never lost, for all her naivete and vivacity, gratified his pride and compelled, upon their second brief visit to New York, even the unqualified approval of his family.

She had inherited all the subtle adaptability of her father's race, nothing of the cold and rigid narrowness of her mother's class. Price had feared that her lively mind might reveal disconcerting shallows, but these little voids were but the divine hiatuses of youth. He sometimes wondered just how strong her character was. There were times when she showed a pronounced inclination for the line of least resistance ... but her youth ... her too sheltered bringing up ... those drab cramped years ... no wonder....

He was glad on the whole that his was the part to mold. Nevertheless, he had his inconsistencies. Unlike many men of strong will and driving purpose he liked strength of character and pronounced individuality in women; and he, too, had had fleeting visions of what life might have been had Flora Thornton entered life twenty years later. He had been quite sincere in telling her that the young stranger reminded him of the most powerful personality he had met in California, and he believed that within a reasonable time Helene would be as variously cultivated, as widely, if less erratically developed. But was there any such insurgent force in her depths? It was not within the possibilities that at any time in her life Flora Thornton had been pliable.

A man had little time to study his wife in California these days. Or at any time? He sometimes wondered. Certainly happy marriages were rare and divorces many. Fine weather nearly all the year round played the deuce with domesticity, and his business could not be neglected for the long vacation abroad to which they both had looked forward so ardently.

Sometimes, even before this vague gray mist had risen between them, he had had moments of wondering whether he knew his wife at all. How could a man know a woman who did not yet know herself? He sighed and wished he had more time to explore the uncharted seas of a woman's soul.

But the cause of the change in her was something far less picturesque, something concrete and sinister. He felt sure of that....

VII

Unless--but that was ridiculous! Impossible!

He sprang to his feet, incredulous, disgusted at the mere thought.

But why not? She was very young, and older and wiser women were afflicted with inconsistencies, little tenacious desires and vanities never quite to be grasped by the elemental male.

He went over to a bookcase containing heavy works of reference and pressed his index finger into the molding. It swung outward, revealing the door of a safe. He manipulated the combination, took from a drawer of the interior a box, opened it and stared at a magnificent Burmah ruby. It was or had been a royal jewel, presented to Masewell Price by one of the great princes of India whose portrait he had painted. The pearls had all been captured long since by Price's sisters and by Morgan V. for his wife; but this ruby his mother had given him as she lay dying. She had bidden him leave it in his father's safe until he was out of college, and then keep it as closely in his personal possession as possible. It would be turned over to him with the rest of his private fortune.

"Never let any woman wear it," she had whispered. "It brings luck to men but not to women. Nothing could have affected my luck one way or the other--I was born to have nothing I wanted, but you, dear little boy. Keep it for your luck and in a safe place, but near you."

He had looked back upon this scene as he grew older as the mere expression of a whim of dissolution, but it had made so deep an impression upon him at the time that insensibly the words sank into his plastic mind creating a superstition that refused to yield to reason. The ruby was Helene's birthstone and she was passionately fond of it. She had begged and coaxed to wear this jewel, and upon one occasion had stamped her little foot and sulked throughout the evening. He had given her a ruby bar, had the clasp of her pearl necklace set with rabies, and last Christmas had presented her with a small but fine "pigeon blood" encircled with diamonds. These had enraptured her for the moment, but she had always circled back to the historic stone, over which her indulgent husband was so unaccountably obstinate.

Until lately. He recalled that for several months she had not mentioned it. Could she have been indulging in a prolonged attack of interior sulks, which affected her spirits, dimmed her radiant personality? He abominated the idea but admitted the possibility. She would not be the first person to be the victim of a secret but furious passion for jewels. He recalled a novel of Hichens; not the matter but the central idea. Authors of other races had used the same motive. Well, if his wife had an abnormal streak in her the sooner he found out the truth the better.

He closed the door of the safe, swung the bookcase into place, slipped the ruby with its curious gold chain that looked massive but hardly weighed an ounce, into his pocket, rang for a servant and told him to ask Mrs. Ruyler to come down to the library as soon as she was dressed.

CHAPTER II

I

Ruyler sighed as he heard his wife walk down the hall. There had been a time when she came running like a child at his summons, but in these days she walked with a leisurely dignity which to his possibly morbid ear betrayed a certain crab-like disposition in her little high heels to slip backward along the polished floor.

She came in smiling, however, and kissed him quickly and warmly. Her extraordinary hair hung down in two long braids, their blue blackness undulating among the soft folds of her thin pink negligee. For the first time Ruyler realized that pink was Helene's favorite color; she seldom wore anything else except white or black, and then always relieved with pink. And why not, with that deep pink blush in her white cheeks, and the velvet blackness of her eyes? People still raved over Helene Ruyler's "coloring," and Price told himself once more as she stood before him, her little head dragged back by the weight of her plaits, her slender throat crossed by a narrow line of black velvet, that he had married one of the most beautiful girls he had ever seen.

He was seized with a sudden sharp pang of jealousy and caught her in his arms roughly, his gray eyes almost as black as hers.

"Tell me," he exclaimed, and the new fear almost choked him, "does any other man interest you--the least little bit?"

She stared at him and then burst into the most natural laugh he had heard from her for months. "That is simply too funny to talk about."

"But I am able to give you so little of my time. Working or tired out at night-

-letting you go out so much alone--but I haven't the heart to insist that you yawn over a book, while I am shut up here, or too fagged to talk even to you. Life is becoming a tragedy for business men--if they've got it in them to care for anything else."

"Well, don't add to the tragedy by cultivating jealousy. I've told you that I am perfectly willing to give up Society and sit like Dora holding your pens--or filling your fountain pen--no, you dictate. What chance has a woman in a business man's life?"

"None, alas, except to look beautiful and be happy. Are you that?--the last I mean, of course!"

She nestled closer to him and laughed again. "More so than ever. To be frank you have completed my happiness by being jealous. I have wondered sometimes if it were a compliment--your being so sure of me."

"That's my idea of love."

"Well, it's mine, too. But if you want me to stay home--"

"Oh, no! You are fond of society? Really, I mean? Why shouldn't you be?--a young thing--"

"What else is there? Of course, I should enjoy it much more if you were always with me. Shall we never have that year in Europe together?"

"God knows. Something is wrong with the world. It needs reorganizing--from the top down. It is inhuman, the way even rich men have to work--to remain rich! But sit down."

He led her over to a chair before the window. The storm was decreasing in violence, the heavy curtain of rain was no longer tossed, but falling in straight intermittent lines, and the islands were coming to life. Even the high and heavy crest of Mount Tamalpais was dimly visible.

"It is the last of the storms, I fancy. Spring is overdue," said Price, who, however, was covertly watching his wife's face. Her color had faded a little, her lids drooped over eyes that stared out at the still turbulent waters.

"I love these San Francisco storms," she said abruptly. "I am so glad we have these few wild months. But Mrs. Thornton has worried and so have we. Her fete at San Mateo comes off on the fourteenth, the first entertainment she has given since her return, and it would be ghastly if it rained. It should be a wonderful sight--those grounds--everybody in fancy dress with little black velvet masks. Don't you think you can go?"

"The fourteenth? I'll try to make it. Who are you to be?"

"Beatrice d'Este--in a court gown of black tissue instead of velvet, with just a touch of pink--oh, but a wonderful creation! I designed it myself. We are not bothering too much about historical accuracy."

"How would you like this for the touch of pink!" He took the immense ruby from his pocket and tossed it into her lap.

For a moment she stared at it with expanding eyes, then gave a little shriek of rapture and flung herself into his arms, the child he had married.

"Is it true? But true? Shall I wear this wonderful thing? The women will die of jealousy. I shall feel like an empress--but more, more, I shall wear this lovely thing--I, I, Helene Ruyler, born Perrin, who never had a franc in her pocket in Rouen! Price! Have you changed your mind--but no! I cannot believe it."

That was it then! He watched her mobile face sharply. It expressed nothing but the excited rapture of a very young woman over a magnificent toy. There was none of the morbid feverish passion he had dreadfully anticipated. His spirits felt lighter, although he sighed that a bauble, even if it were one of the finest of its kind in the world, should have projected its sinister shadow between them. It had a wicked history. But Helene saw no shadows. She held it up to the light, peered into it as it lay half concealed in the cup of her slender white hands, fondled it against her cheek, hung the chain about her neck.

"How I have dreamed of it," she murmured. "How did you come to change your mind?"

"I thought it a pity such a fine jewel should live forever in a safe; and it will become you above all women. Nature must have had you in her eye when she designed the ruby. I had a sudden vision ... and made up my mind that you should wear it the first time I was able to take you to a party. I must keep the letter of my promise."

"And I can only wear it when you are with me?"

"I am afraid so."

"I'm you, if there is anything in the marriage ceremony." Then she kissed him impulsively. "But I won't be a little pig. And I can tell everybody between now and the Thornton fete that I am going to wear it, and I can think and dream of my triumph meanwhile. But why didn't you let me know you were down? It is Sunday, our only day. I overslept shockingly. I didn't get home till two."

"Two? Do you dance until two every night?"

"What else? They lead such a purposeless life out here. We sometimes have classes--but they don't last long. I have almost forgotten that I once had a serious mind. But what would you? It is either society or suffrage. I won't be as serious as that yet. I mean to be young--but young! for five more years. Then I shall become a 'leader,' or vote for the President, or ride on a float in a suffrage parade dressed as the Goddess of Liberty, with my hair down."

He laughed, more and more relieved. "Yes, please remain young until you are twenty-five. By that time I hope the world will have adjusted itself and I shall have the leisure to companion you. Meanwhile, be a child. It is very refreshing to me. Come. I must lock this thing up. I have an interview here with Spaulding in about ten minutes."

She gave it up reluctantly, kissing it much as she had kissed him during their engagement; warm, lingering, but almost impersonal kisses. The ruby seemed miraculously to have restored her beaten youth.

She sat on the edge of a chair as he opened the safe and placed the jewel in its box and drawer.

"There is one other thing I wanted to ask," he said as he rose. "Is your allowance sufficient? It has sometimes occurred to me that you wanted more--for some feminine extravagance."

The light went out of her face. He wondered whimsically if he had locked it in with the ruby, and once more he was conscious that something intangible floated between them. But she looked at him squarely with her shadowed eyes.

"Oh, one could spend any amount, of course, but I really have quite enough."

"You shall have double your present allowance when these cursed times improve. And I have always intended to settle a couple of hundred thousand on you--a quarter of a million--as soon as I could realize without loss on certain investments. But one day I want you to be quite independent."

Her eyes had opened very wide. "A quarter of a million? And it would be all my own? I could do anything with it I liked?"

"Well--I think I should put it in trust. I haven't much faith in the resistance of your sex to tempting investments promising a high rate of interest."

"I have heard you say that when rich men die the amount of worthless stock found in their safe deposit boxes passes belief."

"Quite true. But that is hardly an argument in favor of trusting an even more inexperienced sex with large sums of money."

She laughed, but less naturally than when he had been seized with an unwonted spasm of jealousy. "You will always get the best of me in an argument," she said with her exquisite politeness. "Really, I think I love being wholly dependent upon you. Here comes your detective. What a bore. But at least we lunch together if we do have company. And thank you, thank you a thousand times for promising I shall wear the ruby at last."

She slipped her hand into his for a second, then left the room, smiling over her shoulder, as the locally celebrated "Jake" Spaulding entered. Both Ruyler and his general manager had thought it best to have their cashier watched. There were rumors of gambling and other road house diversions, and they proposed to save their man to the firm, if possible; if not, to discharge him before he followed the usual course and involved Ruyler and Sons in the loss of thousands they could ill afford to spare.

CHAPTER III

I

On the following day Ruyler, who had looked upon the whirlwind of passion that had swept him into a romantic and unworldly marriage, as likely to remain the one brief drama of his prosaic business man's life, began dimly to apprehend that he was hovering on the edge of a sinister and complicated drama whose end he could as little foresee as he could escape from the hand of Fate that was pushing him inexorably forward. When Fate suddenly begins to take a dramatic interest in a man whose course has run like a yacht before a strong breeze, she precipitates him toward one half crisis after another in order to confuse his mental powers and render him wholly a puppet for the final act. These little Earth histrionics are arranged no doubt for the weary gods, who hardly brook a mere mortal rising triumphantly above the malignant moods of the master playwright.

He lunched at the Pacific Union Club and caught the down-town California Street cable car as it passed, finding his favorite seat on the left side of the "dummy" unoccupied. He was thinking of Helene, a little disappointed, but on the whole vastly relieved, congratulating himself that, no longer haunted, he could give his mind wholly to the important question of the merger he contemplated with a rival house that had limped along since the disaster, but had at last manifested its willingness to accept the offer of Ruyler and Sons.

It was a moment before he realized that his mother-in-law occupied the front seat across the narrow space, and even before he recognized that large bulk, he had registered something rigid and tense in its muscles; strained in its attitude. When he raised his eyes to the face he found himself looking at the right cheek instead of the left, and it was pervaded by a sickly green tint quite unlike Madame Delano's florid color. She was listening to a man who sat just behind her on the long seat that ran the length of the dummy. Although the day was clear, there was still a sharp wind and no one else sat outside.

Ruyler knew the man by sight. Before the fire he had owned some of the most disreputable houses in the district the car would pass on its way to the terminus. The buildings were uninsured, and he had made his living since as a detective. Even his political breed had gone out of power in the new San Francisco, but he was well equipped for a certain type of detective work. He had a remarkable memory for faces and could pierce any disguise, he was as persistent as a ferret, and his knowledge of the underworld of San Francisco was illimitable. But his chief assets were that he looked so little like a detective, and that, so secretive were his methods, his calling was practically unknown. He had set up a cheap restaurant with a gambling room behind at which the police winked, although pretending to raid him now and again. He was a large soft man with pendulous cheeks streaked with red, a predatory nose, and a black overhanging mustache. His name was 'Gene Bisbee, and there was a tradition that in his younger days he had been handsome, and irresistible to the women who had made his fortune.

Ruyler was absently wondering what his haughty mother-in-law could have to say to such a man when to his amazement Bisbee planted his elbow in the pillow of flesh just below Madame Delano's neck, and said easily:

"Oh, come off, Marie. I'd know you if you were twenty years older and fifty pounds heavier--and that's going some. Bimmer and two or three others are not so sure--won't bet on it--for twenty years, and, let me see--you weighed about a hundred and thirty-five--perfect figger--in the old days. Must weigh two seventy-five now. That makes one forty-five pounds extra. Well, that and time, and white hair, would change pretty near any woman, particularly one with small features. You look a real old lady, and you can't be mor'n forty-five. How did you manage the white hair? Bleach?"

Ruyler felt his heart turn over. The frozen blood pounded in his brain and distended his own muscles, his mouth unclosed to let his breath escape. Then he became aware that the woman had recovered herself and moved forward, displacing the familiar elbow. She turned imperiously to the motorman.

"Stop at the corner," she said. "And if this man attempts to follow me please send back a policeman. He is intoxicated."

The car stopped at the corner of the street opposite the site of the old Saint Mary's Cathedral, a street where once had been that row of small and evil cottages where French women, painted, scantily dressed in a travesty of the evening gown, called to the passer-by through the slats of old-fashioned green shutters. That had been before Ruyler's day, but he knew the history of the neighborhood, and this man's interest in it. He was not surprised to hear Bisbee laugh aloud as Madame Delano, who stepped off the car with astonishing agility, waddled down the now respectable street. But she held her head majestically and did not look back.

Ruyler squared his back lest the man, glancing over, recognize him. That would be more than he could bear. As the car reached Front Street he sprang from the dummy and walked rapidly north to Ruyler and Sons. He locked himself in his private office, dismissing his stenographer with the excuse that he had important business to think out and must not be disturbed.

II

But business was forgotten. He was as nearly in a state of panic as was possible for a man of his inheritance and ordered life. He belonged to that class of New Yorker that looked with cold disgust upon the women of commerce. So far as he knew he had never exchanged a word with one of them, and had often listened with impatience to the reminiscences of his San Francisco friends, now married and at least intermittently decent, of the famous ladies who once had reigned in the gay night life of San Francisco.

And his mother-in-law! The mother of his wife!

Her name was Marie. In that chaos of flesh an interested eye might discover the ruins of beauty. Her hair, he knew, had been black. He recalled the terror expressed in every line of that mountainous figure--which may well have been perfect twenty years ago. The green pallor of her cheek! And he had long felt, rather than knew, that she possessed magnificent powers of bluff. Her dignified exit had been no more convincing to him than to Bisbee.

He went back over the past and recalled all he knew of the woman whose daughter he had married. She had visited the United States about twenty-one years ago, met and married Delano, and remained in San Francisco two or three months on their way to Japan. Delano had died on the voyage across the Pacific, been buried at sea, and his widow had returned to her family in Rouen and settled down in her brother's household.

This was practically all he knew, for it was all that Helene knew, and Madame Delano never wasted words. It had not occurred to him to question her. Their status in Rouen was established, and if not distinguished it was indubitably respectable and not remotely suggestive of mystery.

Price, convinced that Helene's father must have been a gentleman, recalled that he had asked her one day to tell him something of the Delanos, but his wife had replied vaguely that she believed her mother had been too sad to talk about him for a long while, and then probably had got out of the habit. She knew nothing more than she already had told him.

It came back to him, however, that several times his wife's casual references to the past, and particularly regarding her parents, had not dove-tailed, but that he had dismissed the impression; attributing it to some lapse in his own attention. He had a bad habit of listening and thinking out a knotty business problem at the same time. And there is a curious inhibition in loyal minds which forbids them to put two and two together until suspicion is inescapably aroused.

He had a very well ordered mind, furnished with innumerable little pigeon holes, which flew open at the proper vibration from his admirable memory. He concentrated this memory upon a little bureau of purely personal receptacles and before long certain careless phrases of his wife stood in a neat row.

She had mentioned upon one occasion that she thought she must have been about five when she arrived in Rouen, and remembered her first impression of the Cathedral as well as the boats on the Seine at night. And Cousin Pierre had taken her up the river one Sunday to the church on the height which had been built for a statue of the Virgin that had been excavated there, and bade her kneel and pray at this station for what she wished most. She had prayed for a large wax doll that said papa and mama, and behold, it had arrived the next day.

Madame Delano had told him unequivocally that she had gone directly to Rouen after her husband's death ... but again, although Helene remembered arriving in Rouen with her mother, she must have been left for a time elsewhere, for Helene had another memory--of a convent, where she had tarried for what seemed a very long time to her childish mind. Could she have been sent to a convent from the house in Rouen when she was so little that her memories of that first sojourn were confused? And why? The family had apparently been fond of "la petite Americaine," and even if her devoted mother had been obliged to leave her for several years it is doubtful if they would have sent so young a child to a convent. Rack his memory as he would he could recall no allusion to such a journey, to any separation between mother and child after they were established in Rouen.

But he did remember one of Madame Delano's few references to the past, which might suggest that she had left the child somewhere while she went home to make peace with her family to get her bearings. Her brother had not approved of her marrying an American. "But," she had added graciously, "you see I had no such prejudice. Neither now nor then. James was the best of husbands."

"James!" "Jim."

He had heard the name Jim as he boarded the dummy, uttered in extremely familiar accents; by Bisbee, of course. Yes, and something else. "We all felt bad when he croaked."

His feverishly alert memory darted to another pigeon hole and exhumed another treasure. Some ten or twelve months ago he had been obliged to go to a northern county on business that involved buying up smaller concerns, and would keep him away for a fortnight or more. He had taken Helene, and as they were motoring through one of the old towns she had leaned forward with a little gasp exclaiming:

"How exactly like! If I didn't know that I had never been in California before except merely to be born here I could vow that is where I lived with the dear nuns."

He had asked idly: "Where was your convent?" and she had shaken her head. "Maman says I never was in a convent, that I dreamed it." She had lifted to Ruyler a puzzled face. "I remember she punished me once, when I was about seven and persisted in talking about the convent--I suppose I had forgotten it for a time in the new life, and something brought it back to me. But it is the most vivid memory of my childhood. Do you think I could have been one of those uncanny children that live in a dream world? I hope not. I like to think I am quite normal and full to the brim of common sense." He had laughed and told her not to worry. He had lived in a dream world himself when he was little.

The conviction grew upon him as he sat there that Helene had spent the first five years of her life at the Ursuline Convent in St. Peter. What had her mother-- young and beautiful--been doing during those years, the years of a mother's most anxious devotion and pleasurable interest? He searched his memory for Club reminiscences of a Marie Delano of twenty years earlier, or less. No such name rewarded his mental explorations, and Marie Delano was not a name likely to escape.

He exclaimed aloud at his stupidity. The astute French woman was hardly likely to return to the scene of her former triumphs with an innocent young daughter and an infamous name. Nor, apparently, had she carried it to Rouen after she had manifestly foresworn vice for the sake of her child, even to the length of resigning herself to the dullness of a provincial town.

But "Jim"? Her husband? Could Bisbee have referred to some other Jim who had "croaked" recently? Such women have more than one Jim in their voluminous lives.

Ruyler had that order of mental temperament to which dubiety is the one unendurable condition; he had none of that cowardice which postpones an unpleasant solution until the inevitable moment. Whatever this hideous mystery he would solve it as quickly as possible and then put it out of his life. Beyond question poor Helene was the victim of blackmail; that was the logical explanation of her ill-concealed anxiety--misery, no doubt!

He wished she had had the courage to come directly to him, but it was idle to expect the resolution of a woman of thirty in a child of twenty. It was apparent that she had even tried to shield her mother, for that Madame Delano had been caught unaware to-day was indisputable.

What incredible impudence--or courage?--to return here! There were other resorts in the South and on the Eastern Coast where a pretty girl might reap the harvest of innocent and lovely youth.

Once more his mind abruptly focused itself.

Shortly after his marriage Madame Delano had asked him casually if he could inform her as to the reliability of a certain firm of lawyers, Lawton, Cross and Co. She "thought of buying a ranch," and the firm had been suggested to her by some one or other of these rich people. She also wished to make a will.

He had replied as casually that it was a leading firm, and forgotten the incident promptly. He recalled now that several times he had seen his mother-in-law coming out of the Monadnock Building, where this firm had its offices. He had upon one occasion met her in the lift and she had explained with unaccustomed volubility that she was still thinking of buying a ranch, possibly in Napa County. She understood that quite a fortune might be made in fruit, and it would be a diverting interest for her old age. Possibly she might encourage a favorite nephew to come out and help her run it.

Ruyler, who had been absorbed in his own affairs and hated the sight of any woman during business hours, had felt like telling her that if she wanted to sink her money in a ranch, that was as good a way to get rid of it as any, but had merely nodded and left the elevator. He was not the man to give any one unasked advice and be snubbed for his pains.

If "Jim" was her husband and had "croaked" some two years since, what more natural than that she had been obliged to come to California and settle his estate? Lawton and Cross would keep her secret, as California lawyers, with or without blackmail, had kept many others; perhaps she was an old friend of Lawton's. He had been a "bird" in his time.

Undoubtedly this was the solution. Otherwise she never would have risked the return to San Francisco, even with her changed appearance.

III

It was time to dismiss speculation and proceed to action. He rang up detective headquarters and asked Jake Spaulding to come to him at once.

Spaulding began: "But the matter ain't ripe yet, boss. Nothin' doin' last night--"

But Ruyler cut him short. "Please come immediately--no, not here. Meet me at Long's."

He left the building and walked rapidly to a well-known bar where estimable citizens, even when impervious to the seductions of cocktail and highball, often met in private soundproof rooms to discuss momentous deals, or invoke the aid of detectives whose appearance in home or office might cause the wary bird to fly away.

The detective did not drink, so Ruyler ordered cigars, and a few moments later Spaulding strolled in. His physical movements always belied his nervous keen face. He was the antithesis of 'Gene Bisbee. All honest men compelled to have dealings with him liked and trusted him. A rich man could confide a disgraceful predicament to his keeping without fear of blackmail, and a poor man, if his cause were interesting, might command his services with a nominal fee. He loved the work and regarded himself as an artist, inasmuch as he was exercising a highly cultivated gift, not merely pursuing a lucrative profession. He sometimes longed, it is true, for worthier objects upon which to lavish this gift, and he found them a few years later when the world went to war. He was one of the most valuable men in the Federal Secret Service before the end of 1915.

"What's up?" he asked, as he took possession of the most comfortable chair in the little room and lit a cigar. "You look as if you hadn't slept for a week, and you were lookin' fine yesterday."

"Do you mind if I only half confide in you? It's a delicate matter. I'd like to ask you a few questions and may possibly ask you to find the answer to several others."

"Fire away. Curiosity is not my vice. I'll only call for a clean breast if I find I can't work in the dark."

"Thanks. Do--do you remember any woman of the town named--Marie Delano?" He swallowed hard but brought it out. "Who may have flourished here fifteen or twenty years ago?"

Spaulding knew that Ruyler's wife had been named Delano, but he refrained from whistling and fixed his sharp honest blue eyes on the opposite wall.

"Nope. Sounds fancy enough, but she was no Queen of the Red Light District in S.F."

"I was convinced she could not have been known under that name. Do you know of any woman of that sort who was married--possibly--to a man whose first name was James--Jim--and who left abruptly, while she was still young and hand-some, just about fifteen years ago?"

"Lord, that's a poser! Do you mean to say she married and retired--landed some simp? They do once in a while. Could tell you queer things about certain ancestries in this old town."

"No--I don't think that was it. I have reason to think she had been married for at least six years before she left. Can't you think of any Marie who was married to a Jim--in--in that class of life?"

"I was pretty much of a kid fifteen years ago, but I can recall quite a few Maries and even more Jims. But the Jims were much too wary to marry the Maries. Try it again, partner. Let us approach from another angle. What did your Marie look like?"

"She must have been tall--uncommonly tall--with black hair and small fea-tures; black eyes that must have been large at that time. I--I--believe she had a very fine figure."

"What nationality?"

"French."

The detective recrossed his legs. "French. Oh, Lord! The town was fairly over-run with them. Made you think there was nothing in all this talk about gay Paree. All the ladybirds seemed to have taken refuge here. You have no idea of her last name!"

"It might have been Perrin."

"Never. Not after she got here and set up in business. More likely Lestrange or Delacourt--"

"Was there a Delacourt?"

"Not that I remember. I don't see light anywhere. Of course it won't take me twenty-four hours to get hold of the history and appearance of every queen who was named Marie fifteen years ago, and your description helps a lot. Records were burned, but some of the older men on the force are walking archives. For the matter of that you might draw out some old codger in your club and get as much as I can give you--"

"Rather not! I think I'll have to give you my confidence."

"Much the shortest and straightest route. Just fancy you're takin' a nasty dose of medicine for the good of your health. I guess this is a case where I can't work in the dark."

"Have you ever noticed an elderly woman, seated in the court of the Palace Hotel--immensely stout?"

"I should say I had. One of the sights of S.F. Why--of course--she's your mother-in-law!"

"Has there been any talk about her!"

"Some comment on her size. And her childlike delight in watchin' the show."

"Nothing else? No one has claimed to recognize her?"

Spaulding sat up straight, his nose pointing. "Recognize her? What d'you mean?"

"I mean that I overheard a conversation--one-sided--to-day on the California Street dummy, in which Bisbee accused Madame Delano practically of what I have told you. At least that is the way I interpreted it. He called her Marie, alluded in an unmistakable manner to a disgraceful past in which he had known her intimately, and was confident that he recognized her in spite of her flesh and white hair. I am positive that she recognized him, although she was clever enough not to reply."

"Jimminy! The plot thickens. That scoundrel never forgot a face in his life. I don't train with him--not by a long sight--so if there's been any talk in his bunch, I naturally wouldn't have heard it. You say her name is Marie now?"

"Yes."

"And Perrin is her real name?"

"She comes of a well-known family of Rouen of that name. She lived there with her child for at least thirteen years before her return to California. Of that I am certain. Her daughter is now twenty. I wish to know where she kept that child during the first five years of its life. I have reason to think it was in the Ursuline Convent at St. Peter."

"That's easy settled. And you think the father's first name was Jim?"

"She told me that his name was James Delano. Also that he died within the first year of their marriage, when the child was two months old, during the voyage to Japan. That may be, but I can see no reason for her returning here unless he died more recently and the settlement of his estate demanded her presence."

"Pretty good reasoning, particularly if you are sure she stayed here until the child was five. Some of them have pretty decent instincts. She may have made up her mind to give the kid a chance, and returned to her relations. Of course we must assume that they knew nothing of her life."

"I am positive they did not. But there had been some sort of estrangement. I have been given to understand that it was because she married an American. Of course she may not have written to them at all for six or seven years. Her story is that she was visiting other relatives in a place called Holbrook Centre, Vermont, and met this man and married him. Then that he was detained by business in San Francisco for several months, and the child born here."

"Good commonplace story. Just the sort that is never questioned. Of course if she did not correspond with her family during all that time she could adopt any name for her return to respectability that she chose. Delano wasn't it? That's certain. What line do you intend to take? After I've delivered the facts?"

"My object is to have the child's legitimacy established, if possible, then see that Madame Delano leaves California forever. I think that she could be terrified by a threat of blackmail. I can't imagine the mere chance of recognition worrying her, for I should say she had as much courage as presence of mind. But her passion is money. If she thought there was any danger of being forced to hand over what she has I fancy she would get out as quickly as possible. She is an intelligent woman and I imagine she has taken a sardonic pleasure in sitting out in full view of San Francisco, and getting away with it."

"And marrying her girl to the greatest catch in California," thought the detective, but he said:

"I believe you're dead right, although, of course, there may be nothing in it. Even 'Gene Bisbee might be mistaken, pryin' a gazelle out of an elephant like that. Now, tell me all you know."

When Ruyler had covered every point Spaulding nodded. "It's possible this Jim was the maquereau and she made him marry her for the sake of the child. Doubt if the date can be proved except through the lawyers, and it will be hard to make them talk. Of course if there is a Holbrook Centre and she was married there--but I have my doubts. The point is that he evidently married her if she is settlin' up his estate. I'll find out what Jims have died within the last three years or so. That's easy. The direct route to the one we want is through St. Peter. I'll go up to-night."

"And you'll report to-morrow?"

"Yep. Meet me here at six P.M. Lucky the man seems to have died after the fire. I'll set some one on the job of searching death records right away."

CHAPTER IV

I

Ruyler had half promised to go to a dinner that night at the house of John Gwynne, whose wife would chaperon his wife afterward to the last of the Assembly dances.

Gwynne was his English friend who had abandoned the ancient title inherited untimely when he was making a reputation in the House of Commons, and become an American citizen in California, where he had a large ranch originally the property of an American grandmother. His migration had been justified in his own eyes by his ready adaptation to the land of his choice and to the opportunities offered in the rebuilding of San Francisco after the earthquake and fire, as well as in the renovation of its politics. He had made his ranch profitable, read law as a stepping-stone to the political career, and had just been elected to Congress. Ruyler was one of his few intimate friends and had promised to go to this farewell dinner if possible. A place would be kept vacant for him until the last minute.

Gwynne had married Isabel Otis[1], a Californian of distinguished beauty and abilities, whose roots were deep in San Francisco, although she had "run a ranch" in Sonoma County. The Gwynnes and the Thorntons until Ruyler met Helene had been the friends whose society he had sought most in his rare hours of leisure, and he had spent many summer week-ends at their country homes. He had hoped that the intimacy would deepen after his marriage, but Helene during the past year had gone almost exclusively with the younger set, the "dancing squad"; natural enough considering her age, but Ruyler would have expected a girl of so much intelligence,

---

1   See "Ancestors."

to say nothing of her severe education, to have tired long since of that artificial wing of society devoted solely to froth, and gravitated naturally toward the best the city afforded. But she had appeared to like the older women better at first than later, although she accepted their invitations to large dinners and dances.

Ruyler made up his mind to attend this dinner at Gwynne's, and telephoned his acceptance before he left Long's. Business or no business, he should be his wife's bodyguard hereafter. There were blackmailers in society as out of it, and it was possible that his ubiquity would frighten them off. Whether to demand his wife's confidence or not he was undecided. Better let events determine.

II

When he arrived at home he went directly to Helene's room, but paused with his hand on the knob of the door. He heard his mother-in-law's voice and she was the last person he wished to meet until he was in a position to tell her to leave the country. He was turning away impatiently when Madame Delano lifted her hard incisive tones.

"And you promised me!" she exclaimed passionately. "I trusted you, I never believed--"

Price retreated hurriedly to his own room, and it was not until he had taken a cold shower and was half dressed that he permitted himself to think.

That wretch had known, then! It was she who had been blackmailing her daughter. And the poor child had been afraid to confide in him, to ask him for money. No wonder her eyes had flashed at the prospect of a fortune of her own....

An even less welcome ray illuminated his mind at this point. His wife was not unversed in the arts of dissimulation herself. True, she was French and took naturally to diplomatic wiles; true, also, the instinct of self-preservation in even younger members of a sex that man in his centuries of power had made, superficially, the weaker, was rarely inert.

What woman would wish her husband to know disgraceful ancestral secrets which were no fault of hers? A much older woman would not be above entombing them, if the fates were kind. But it saddened him to think that his wife should be rushed to maturity along the devious way. Poor child, he must win her confidence as quickly as his limping wits would permit and shift her burden to his own shoulders.

Having learned through the medium of the house telephone that his mother-in-law had departed, he knocked at his wife's door. She opened it at once and there was no mark of agitation on her little oval face under its proudly carried crown of heavy braids. She was looking very lovely in a severe black velvet gown whose texture and depth cunningly matched her eyes and threw into a relief as artful the white purity of her skin and the delicate pink of lip and cheek.

She smiled at him brilliantly. "It can't be true that you are going with me?"

"I've reformed. I shall go with you everywhere from this time forth. But I thought I heard your mother's voice when I came in--"

"She often comes in about dressing time to see me in a new frock. How heavenly that you will always go with me." Her voice shook a little and she leaned over to smooth a possible wrinkle in her girdle.

"Will you come down to the library? We are rather early."

He went directly to the safe and took out the ruby and clasped the chain about her neck. The chain was long and the great jewel took a deeper and more mysterious color from the somber background of her bodice.

Helene gasped. "Am I to wear it to-night? That would be too wonderful. This is the last great night in town."

"Why not? I shall be there to mount guard. You shall always wear it when I am able to go out with you."

She lifted her radiant face, although it remained subtly immobile with a new and almost formal self-possession. "I am even more delighted than I was yesterday, for at the fete there will be so much novelty to distract attention. You always think of the nicest possible things."

When they were in the taxi he put his arm about her.

"I wonder," he began gropingly, "if you would mind not going out when I cannot go with you? I'll go as often as I can manage. There are reasons--"

He felt her light body grow rigid. "Reasons? You told me only yesterday--"

"I know. But I have been thinking it over. That is rather a fast lot you run with. I know, of course, they are F.F.C.'s, and all the rest of it, but if I ever drove up to the Club House in Burlingame in the morning and saw you sitting on the veranda smoking and drinking gin fizzes--"

"You never will! I could not swallow a gin fizz, or any nasty mixed drink. And although I have had my cigarette after meals ever since I was fifteen, I never smoke in public."

"I confess I cannot see you in the picture that rose for some perverse reason in my mind; but--well, you really are too young to go about so much without your husband--"

"I am always chaperoned to the large affairs. Mrs. Gwynne takes me to the Fairmont to-night."

"I know. But scandal is bred in the marrow of San Francisco. Its social history is founded upon it, and it is almost a matter of principle to replace decaying props. Do you mind so much not going about unless I can be with you?"

"No, of course not." Her voice was sweet and submissive, but her body did not relax. She added graciously: "After all, there are so many luncheons, and we often dance in the afternoon."

He had not thought of that! What avail to guard her merely in the evening? It was not her life that was in danger....

And he seemed as immeasurably far from obtaining her confidence as before. He had always understood that the ways of matrimonial diplomacy were strewn with pitfalls and wished that some one had opened a school for married men before his time.

He made another clumsy attempt. The cab was swift and had almost covered the long distance between the Western Addition and Russian Hill. "Other things have worried me. You are so generous. Society here as elsewhere has its parasites, its dead beats, trying to limp along by borrowing, gambling, 'amusing,' doing dirty work of various sorts. It has worried me lest one or more of these creatures may have tried to impose on you with hard luck tales--borrow--"

She laughed hysterically. "Price, you are too funny! I do lend occasionally--to the girls, when their allowance runs out before the first of the month; but I don't know any dead beats."

He plunged desperately. "Your mother's voice sounded rather agitated for her. Of course I did not stop to listen, but it occurred to me that she may have been gambling in stocks, or have got into some bad land deal. She is so confoundedly close-mouthed--if she wants money send her to me."

Helene sat very straight. Her little aquiline profile against the passing street lights was as aloof as imperial features on an ancient coin.

"Really, Price, I don't think you can be as busy as you pretend if you have time to indulge in such flights of imagination. Maman has never tried to borrow a penny of me, and she is the last person on earth to gamble in stocks or any thing else. Or to buy land except on expert advice. I think she has given up that idea, anyhow. She said this evening she thought it was time for her to visit our people in Rouen."

"Oh, she did! Helene, I must tell you frankly that I heard her reproach you for having broken a promise, and she spoke with deep feeling."

It was possible that the Roman profile turned white, but in the dusk of the car he could not be sure. His wife, however, merely shrugged her shoulders and replied calmly:

"My dear Price, if that has worried you, why didn't you say so at once? I am rather ashamed to tell you, all the same. Maman has been at me lately to persuade you to let her have the ruby for a week. She is dreadfully superstitious, poor maman, and is convinced it would bring her some tremendous good fortune--"

"I have never met a woman who, I could swear, was freer from superstition--"

Price closed his lips angrily. Of what use to tax her feminine defenses further? He had known her long enough to be sure she would rather tell the truth than lie. It was evident that she had no intention of lowering her barriers, and he must play the game from the other end: get the proof he needed and engineer his mother-in-law out of the United States.

Some time, however, he would have it out with his wife. Being a business man and always alert to outwit the other man, he wanted neither intrigue nor mystery in his home, but a serene happiness founded upon perfect confidence. He found it impossible to remain appalled or angry at his wife's readiness of resource in guarding a family secret that must have shocked the youth in her almost out of existence.

He patted her hand, and felt its chill within the glove.

"It was like you never to have mentioned it," he murmured. "For, of course, it is quite impossible."

"That is what I told her decidedly to-night, and I do not think she will ask again. It hurts me to refuse dear maman anything. Her devotion to me has been wonderful--but wonderful," she added on a defiant note.

"A mother's devotion, particularly to a girl of your sort, does not make any call upon my exclamation points. But here we are."

*   *   *   *   *

The car rolled up the graded driveway Gwynne had built for the old San Francisco house that before his day had been approached by an almost perpendicular flight of wooden steps. They were late and the company had assembled: the Thorntons, Trennahans, and eight or ten young people, all of whom would be chaperoned by the married women to the dance at the Fairmont.

Russian Hill had escaped the fire, but Nob Hill had been burnt down to its bones, and the Thorntons and Trennahans had not rebuilt, preferring, like many others, to live the year round in their country homes and use the hotels in winter.

The moment Helene entered the drawing-room it was evident that the ruby was to make as great a sensation as the soul of woman could desire. Even the older people flocked about her and the girls were frank and shrill in their astonishment and rapture.

"Helene! Darling! The duckiest thing--I never saw anything so perfectly dandy and wonderful! I'd go simply mad! Do, just let me touch it! I could eat it!"

Mrs. Thornton, who at any time scorned to conceal envy, or pretend indifference, looked at the great burning stone with a sigh and turned to her husband.

"Why didn't you manage to get it for me?" she demanded. "It would be far more suitable--a magnificent stone like that!--on me than on that baby."

"My darling," murmured Ford anxiously, "I never laid eyes on the thing before, or on one like it. I'll find out where Ruyler got it, and try--"

"Do you suppose I'd come out with a duplicate? You should have thought of it years ago. You always promised to take me to India."

"It should be on you!" He gazed at her adoringly. Her hair was dressed in a high and stately fashion to-night. She wore a gown of gold brocade and a necklace and little tiara of emeralds and diamonds; she was looking very handsome and very regal. Thornton was a thin, dark, nervous wisp of a man, who had borne his share of the burdens laid upon his city in the cataclysm of 1906, but if his wife had demanded an enormous historic ruby he would have done his best to gratify her. But how the deuce could a man--

Mrs. Gwynne was holding the stone in her hand and smiling into its flaming depths without envy. She was one of those women of dazzling white skin, black hair and blue eyes, who, when wise, never wear any jewels but pearls. She wore the Gwynne pearls to-night and a shimmering white gown.

Ruyler glanced round the fine old room with the warm feeling of satisfaction he always experienced at a San Francisco function, where the women were almost as invariably pretty as they were gay and friendly. He did not like the younger men he met on these occasions as well as he did many of the older ones; the serious ones would not waste their time on society, and there were too many of the sort who were asked everywhere because they had made a cult of fashion, whether they could afford it or not. A few were the sons of wealthy parents, and were more dissipated than those obliged to "hold down" a job that provided them with money enough above their bare living expenses to make them useful and presentable.

Ruyler looked upon both sorts as cumberers of the earth, and only tolerated them in his own house when his wife gave a party and dancing men must be had at any price.

There was one man here to-night for whom he had always held particular detestation. His name was Nicolas Doremus. He was a broker in a small way, but Ruyler guessed that he made the best part of his income at bridge, possibly poker. He lived with two other men in a handsome apartment in one of the new buildings that were changing the old skyline of San Francisco. His dancing teas and suppers were admirably appointed and the most exclusive people went to them.

Ruyler knew his history in a general way. His father had made a fortune in "Con. Virginia" in the Seventies, and his mother for a few years had been the social equal of the women who now patronized her son. But unfortunately the gambling microbe settled down in Harry Doremus' veins, and shortly after his son was born he engaged his favorite room at the Cliff House and blew out his brains. His wife was left with a large house, which as a last act of grace he had forborne to mortgage and made over to her by deed. She immediately advertised for boarders, and as her cooking was excellent and she had the wit to drop out of society and give her undivided attention to business, she prospered exceedingly.

She concentrated her ambitions upon her only child; sent him to a private school patronized by the sons of the wealthy, and herself taught him every ingratiating social art. She wanted him to go to college, but by this time "Nick" was nineteen and as highly developed a snob as her maternal heart had planned. Knowing that he must support himself eventually, he was determined to begin his business career at once, and believed, with some truth, that there was a prejudice in this broad field against college men. He entered the brokerage firm of a bachelor who had occupied Mrs. Doremus' best suite for fifteen years, and made a satisfactory clerk, the while he cultivated his mother's old friends.

When Mrs. Doremus died he sold the house and good will for a considerable sum, and, combining it with her respectable savings, formed a partnership with two other young fellows, whose fathers were rich, but old-fashioned enough to insist that their sons should work. Nick did most of the work. His partners, during the rainy season, sat with their feet on the radiator and read the popular magazines, and in fine weather upheld the outdoor traditions of the state.

The firm had a slender patronage, as Ruyler happened to know, but Doremus was a member of the Pacific Union Club, and although he dined out every night, he must have spent six or seven thousand a year. It was amiably assumed that his social services,--he played and sang and often entertained exacting groups throughout an entire evening--his fetching and carrying for one rich old lady, accounted for his ability to keep out of debt and pay for his many extravagances; but Ruyler knew that he was principally esteemed at the small green table, and he vaguely recalled as he looked over his head to-night that he had heard disconnected murmurs of less honorable sources of revenue.

As Ruyler turned away with a frown he met Gwynne's eyes traveling from the same direction. "I didn't ask him," he said apologetically. "Hate men too well dressed. Looks as if he posed for tailors' ads in the weeklies. Never could stand the social parasite anyhow, but Aileen Lawton asked Isabel to let her bring him, as they are going to open the ball to-night with some new kind of turkey trot.

"Glad I'm off for Washington. California's the greatest place on earth in the dry season, but I'd have passed few winters here if it hadn't been for the work we all had to do, and even then it would have been heavy going without my wife's companionship."

Ruyler sighed. Should he ever enjoy his wife's companionship? And into what sort of woman would she develop if forced along crooked ways by ugly secrets, blackmail, perpetual lying and deceit? He longed impatiently for the decisive interview with Spaulding on the morrow. Then, at least he could prepare for action, and, after all, even of more importance now than winning his wife's confidence and saving her from mental anguish, was the averting of a scandal that would echo across the continent straight into the ears of his half-reconciled father.

III

It was about halfway through dinner that the primitive man in him routed every variety of apprehension that had tormented him since two o'clock that afternoon.

Trennahan, another distinguished New Yorker, who had made his home in California for many years, had taken in Mrs. Gwynne, and his Spanish California wife sat at the foot of the table with the host. Ford had been given a lively girl, Aileen Lawton, to dissipate the financial anxieties of the day, and, to Ruyler's satisfaction, Mrs. Thornton had fallen to his lot and he sat on the left of Isabel. In this little group at the head of the table, his chosen intimates, who were more interested in the affairs of the world than in Consummate California, Ruyler had forgotten his wife for a time and had not noticed with whom she had gone in to dinner.

But during an interval when Mrs. Thornton's attention had been captured by the man on her right, and the others drawn into a discussion over the merits of the new mayor, Price became aware that Doremus sat beside his wife halfway down the table on the opposite side, and that they were talking, if not arguing, in a low tone, oblivious for the moment of the company.

The deferential bend was absent from the neck of the adroit social explorer, his head was alertly poised above the lovely young matron whose beauty, wealth, and foreign personality, to say nothing of the importance of her husband, gave her something of the standing of royalty in the aristocratic little republic of San Francisco Society. There was a vague threat in that poise, as if at any moment venom might dart down and strike that drooping head with its crown of blue-black braids. Suddenly Helene lifted her eyes, full of appeal, to the round pale blue orbs that at this moment openly expressed a cold and ruthless mind.

Ruyler endeavored to piece together those disconnected whispers--letters discovered or stolen--blackmail--but such whispers were too often the whiffs from energetic but empty minds, always floating about and never seeming to bring any culprit to book.

Had this man got hold of his wife's secret?

But this merely sequacious thought was promptly routed. The young man, who was undeniably good looking and was rumored to possess a certain cold charm for women--although, to be sure, the wary San Francisco heiress had so far been impervious to it--was now leaning over Mrs. Price Ruyler with a coaxing possessive air, and the appeal left Helene's eyes as she smiled coquettishly and began to talk with her usual animation; but still in a tone that was little more than a murmur.

She moved her shoulder closer to the man she evidently was bent upon fascinating, and her long eyelashes swept up and down while her black eyes flashed and her pink color deepened.

There was a faint amusement mixed with Doremus' habitual air of amiable deference, and somewhat more of assurance, but he was as absorbed as Helene and had no eyes for Janet Maynard, on his left, whose fortune ran into millions.

For a moment Ruyler, who had kept his nerve through several years of racking strain which, even an American is seldom called upon to survive, wondered if he were losing his mind. To business and all its fluctuations and even abnormalities, he had been bred; there was probably no condition possible in the world of finance and commerce which could shatter his self-possession, cloud his mental processes. But his personal life had been singularly free of storms. Even his emotional upheaval, when he had fallen completely in love for the first time, had lacked that torment of uncertainty which might have played a certain havoc, for a time, with those quick unalterable decisions of the business hour; and even his engagement had only lasted a month.

It was true that during the past six months he had worried off and on about the shadow that had fallen upon his wife's spirits and affected his own, but, when he had had time to think of it, before yesterday morning, he had assumed it was due to some phase of feminine psychology which he had never mastered. That she could be interested in another man never had crossed his mind, in spite of his passing flare of jealousy. She was still passionately in love with, him, for all her vagaries--or so he had thought--

Ruyler was conscious of a riotous confusion of mind that really made him apprehensive. Had he witnessed that scene on the dummy--this afternoon?--it seemed a long while ago--had he heard those portentous words of his mother-in-law to his wife?--had they meant that she had warned her daughter against the bad blood in her veins, extracted a promise--broken!--to walk in the narrow way of the dutiful wife--mercifully spared by a fortunate marriage the terrible temptations of the older woman's youth? Had Helene confessed ... in desperate need of help, advice? ... Doremus was just the bounder to compromise a woman and then blackmail her.... Good God! What *was* it?

For all his mental turmoil he realized that here alone was the only possible menace to his life's happiness. His mother-in-law's past was a bitter pill for a proud man to swallow, and there was even the possibility of his wife's illegitimacy, but, after all, those were matters belonging to the past, and the past quickly receded to limbo these days.

Even an open scandal, if some one of the offal sheets of San Francisco got hold of the story and published it, would be forgotten in time. But this--if his wife had fallen in love with another man--and women had no discrimination where love was concerned--(if a decent chap got a lovely girl it was mainly by luck; the rotters got just as good)--then indeed he was in the midst of disaster without end. The present was chaos and the future a blank. He'd enlist in the first war and get himself shot....

Helene had a charming light coquetry, wholly French, and she exercised it indiscriminately, much to the delight of the old beaux, for she loved to please, to be admired; she had an innocent desire that all men should think her quite beautiful and irresistible. Even her husband had never seen her in an unbecoming *deshabille*; she coquetted with him shamelessly, whenever she was not too gloriously serious and intent only upon making him happy. Until lately--

This was by no means her ordinary form.

He had come upon too many couples in remote corners of conservatories, had been a not unaccomplished principal in his own day ... there was, beyond question, some deep understanding between her and this man.

Suddenly Ruyler's gaze burned through to his wife's consciousness. She moved her eyes to his, flushed to her hair, then for a moment looked almost gray. But she recovered herself immediately and further showed her remarkable powers of self-possession by turning back to her partner and talking to him with animation instead of plunging into conversation with the man on her right.

At the same moment Ruyler became subtly aware that Mrs. Thornton was looking at his wife and Doremus, and as his eyes focused he saw her long, thin, mobile mouth curl and her eyes fill with open disdain. The mist in his brain fled as abruptly as an inland fog out in the bay before one of the sudden winds of the Pacific. In any case, his mind hardly could have remained in a state of confusion for long; but that his young wife was being openly contemned by the cleverest as well as the most powerful woman in San Francisco was enough to restore his equilibrium in a flash. Whatever his wife's indiscretions, it was his business to protect her until such time as he had proof of more than indiscretion. And in this instance he should be his own detective.

He turned to Mrs. Thornton.

"Going on to the Fairmont?" he asked.

"Oh, yes, I have a new gown--have you admired it? Arrived from Paris last night--and I am chaperoning two of these girls. You are not, of course?"

"I did intend to, but it's no go. Still, I may drop in late and take my wife home--"

"Let me take her home." Was his imagination morbid, or was there something both peremptory and eager in Mrs. Thornton's tones? "I'm stopping at the Fairmont, of course, but Fordy and I often take a drive after a hot night and a heavy supper."

"If you would take her home in case I miss it. I must go to the office--"

"I'd like to. That's settled." This time her tones were warm and friendly. Ruyler knew that Mrs. Thornton did not like his wife, but her friendliness toward him, since her return from Europe three or four months ago, had increased, if anything. His mind was now working with its accustomed keen clarity. He recalled that there had been no surprise mixed with the contempt in her regard of his wife and Doremus.... He also recalled that several times of late when he had met her at the

Fairmont--where he often lunched with a group of men--she had regarded him with a curious considering glance, which he suddenly vocalized as: "How long?"

This affair had been going on for some time, then. Either it was common talk, or some circumstance had enlightened Mrs. Thornton alone.

He glanced around the table. No one appeared to be taking the slightest notice of one of many flirtations. At least, whatever his wife's infatuation, he could avert gossip. Mrs. Thornton might be a tigress, but she was not a cat.

"When do you go down to Burlingame?" she asked.

"Not for two or three weeks yet. I don't fancy merely sleeping in the country. But by that time things will ease up a bit and I can get down every day in time to have a game of golf before dinner."

"Shall Mrs. Ruyler migrate with the rest?"

"Hardly."

"It will be dull for her in town. No reflections on your charming society, but of course she does not get much of it, and she will miss her young friends. After all, she is a child and needs playmates."

Ruyler darted at her a sharp look, but she was smiling amiably. Doremus and the men he lived with, in town had a bungalow at Burlingame and they bought their commutation tickets at precisely the fashionable moment. "She will stay in town," he said shortly. "She needs a rest, and San Francisco is the healthiest spot on earth."

"But trying to the nerves when what we inaccurately call the trade winds begin. Why not let her stay with me? Of course she would be lonely in her own house, and is too young to stay there alone anyhow, but I'd like to put her up, and you certainly could run down week-ends--possibly oftener. American men are always obsessed with the idea that they are twice as busy as they really are."

"You are too good. I'll put it up to Helene. Of course it is for her to decide. I'd like it mighty well." But grateful as he was, his uneasiness deepened at her evident desire to place her forces at his disposal.

CHAPTER V

I

A nd you won't take me to the party?" Helene pouted charmingly as her husband laid her pink taffeta wrap over her shoulders. "I thought you said you might make it, and it would be too delightful to dance with you once more."

"I'm afraid not. The Australian mail came in just as business closed and it's on my mind. I want to go over it carefully before I dictate the answers in the morning, and that means two or three hours of hard work that will leave me pretty well fagged out. Mrs. Thornton has offered to take you home."

"I hate her."

"Oh, please don't!" Ruyler smiled into her somber eyes. "She wants the drive, and it would be taking the Gwynnes so far out of the way. Mrs. Thornton very kindly suggested it."

"I hate her," said Helene conclusively. "I wish now I'd kept my own car. Then I could always go home alone."

"You shall have a car next winter. And this time I shall not permit you to pay for it out of your allowance--which in any case I hope to increase by that time."

Her eyes flamed, but not with anger. "Then I'll sell my electric to Aileen Lawton right away. We have the touring car in the country, and she has been trying to make her father buy her an electric--"

"I'm afraid you'll be disappointed in your bargain. Second-hand cars, no matter what their condition, always go at a sacrifice, and old Lawton is a notorious screw. Better not let it go for two or three hundreds; you look very sweet driving about in it.... Oh, by the way--I had forgotten." He slipped his hand under her coat, unfastened the chain and slipped the jewel into his pocket. "I am sorry," he said, with real contrition, "and almost wish I had forgotten the thing; but I am a little superstitious about keeping that old promise."

She laughed. "And yet you will not permit poor maman a little superstition of her own! But I am rather glad. Everybody at the ball will hear of the ruby, and I shall be able to keep them in suspense until the Thornton fete. Good night. Don't work too hard. Couldn't you get there for supper?"

"'Fraid not."

II

He did go down to the office and glance through the Australian mail, but at a few moments before twelve he took a California Street car up to the Fairmont Hotel and went directly to the ballroom. Mrs. Thornton was standing just within the doorway, but came toward him with lifted eyebrows.

"This is like old times," she said playfully.

"I found less mail than I expected and thought I would come and have a dance with my wife." His eyes wandered over the large room, gayly decorated, and filled with dancing couples.

Mrs. Thornton laughed. "A belle like your wife? She is always engaged for every dance on her program before she is halfway down this corridor."

"Oh, well, husbands have some rights. I'll take it by force. I don't see her--she must be sitting out."

Mrs. Thornton slipped her arm through his. "This dance has just begun. Walk me up and down. I am tired of standing on one foot."

They strolled down the corridor and through the large central hall. Older folks sat or stood in groups; a few young couples were sitting out. Ruyler did not see his wife, and concluded she had been resting at the moment in the dowager ranks against the wall of the ballroom. The music ceased sooner than he expected and Mrs. Thornton, who had been talking with animation on the subject of several fine pictures she had bought while abroad for the Museum in Golden Gate Park, including one by Masefield Price, broke off with an impatient exclamation: "Bother! I must run up to my room at once and telephone. Wait for me here."

She steered him toward a group of men. "Mr. Gwynne, keep Mr. Ruyler from causing a riot in the ballroom. He insists upon dancing with his wife. Hold him by force."

They were standing near the staircase and some distance from the lift. Mrs. Thornton ran up the stairs, pausing for an irresistible moment and looking down at the company. As she stood there, poised, she looked a royal figure with her cloth of gold train covering the steps below her and her high and flashing head. "Wait for me," she said, imperiously to Price. "I cannot meander down that corridor, deserted and alone."

Ruyler smiled at her, but said to Gwynne: "I'll just go and engage my wife for a dance and be back in a jiffy--"

Gwynne clasped his hand about Ruyler's arm. "Just a moment, old chap. I want your opinion--"

"But there is the music again. I'll be knocking people over--"

"You will if you go now, and there'll be dancing for hours yet. Your wife has been dividing up--now, tell me if you back me in this proposition or not. I'm going to Washington to represent you fellows--"

But Ruyler had broken politely away and was walking down the long corridor. When he arrived at the ballroom he saw at a glance that his wife was not there, for the floor was only half filled. But there were other rooms where dancers sat in couples or groups when tired. He went hastily through all of them, but saw nothing of his wife. Nor of Doremus.

Mrs. Thornton had gone in search of her.

And Gwynne knew.

This time the hot blood was pounding in his head. He felt as he imagined mad-men did when about to run amok. Or quite as primitive as any Californian of the surging "Fifties."

He was in one of the smaller rooms and he sat down in a corner with his back to the few people in it and endeavored to take hold of himself; the conventional training of several lifetimes and his own intense pride forbade a scene in public. But his curved fingers longed for Doremus' throat and he made up his mind that if his awful suspicions were vindicated he would beat his wife black and blue. That was far more sensible and manly than running whining to a divorce court.

The effort at self-control left him gasping, but when he rose from his shelter he was outwardly composed, and determined to seek Gwynne and force the truth from him. He would not discuss his wife with another woman. And whatever this hideous tragedy brooding over his life he would go out and come to grips with it at once.

III

And in the corridor he saw his wife chatting gayly with a group of young friends. Her color was paler than usual, perhaps, but that was not uncommon at a party, and otherwise she was as unruffled, as normal in appearance and manner, as when they had parted at the Gwynnes'.

Nevertheless, he went directly up to her, and as she gave a little cry of pleased surprise, he drew her hand through his arm. "Come!" he said imperiously. "You are to dance this with me. I broke away on purpose--"

"But, darling, I am full up--"

"You have skipped at least two. I have been looking everywhere for you--"

"Polly Roberts dragged me upstairs to see the new gowns M. Dupont brought her from Paris. They came this afternoon--so did Mrs. Thornton's--but of course I'll dance this with you. You don't look well," she added anxiously. "Aren't you?"

"Quite, but rather tired--mentally. I need a dance...."

He wondered if she had gently propelled him down the corridor. They were some distance from the group. It was impossible for him to go back and ask if his wife's story were true. Mrs. Thornton was nowhere to be seen, neither in the corridor nor in the ballroom. Nor was Doremus. He set his teeth grimly and managed to smile down upon his wife.

"I shall insist upon having more than one," he said gallantly. "At least three hesitations."

She drew in her breath with a mock sigh and swept from under her long lashes a glance that still had the power to thrill him. "Outrageous, but I shall try to bear up," and the next moment they were giving a graceful exhibition of the tango.

"I don't see your friend Doremus," he said casually, as he stood fanning her at the end of the dance.

She lifted her eyebrows haughtily. "My friend? That parasite?"

"You seemed very friendly at dinner."

"I usually am with my dinner companion. One's hostess is to be considered. Oh--I remember--he was telling me some very amusing gossip, although he teased me into fearing he wouldn't. Now, if you are going to dance this hesitation with me you had better whirl me off. It is Mr. Thornton's, and I see him coming."

Ruyler did not see Doremus until supper was half over and then the young man entered the dining-room hurriedly, his usually serene brow lowering and his lips set. He walked directly up to Helene.

"Beastly luck!" he exclaimed. "Hello, Ruyler. Didn't know you honored parties any more. I had to break away to meet the Overland train--beastly thing was late, of course. Then I had to take them to five hotels before I could settle them. They had two beastly little dogs and the hotels wouldn't take them in and they wouldn't give up the dogs. Some one ought to set up a high-class dog hotel. Sure it would pay. But you'll give me the first after supper, won't you?"

Helene gave him a casual smile that was a poor reward for his elaborate apology. "So sorry," she said with the sweet distant manner in which she disposed of bores and climbers, "but Mr. Ruyler and I are both tired. We are going home directly after supper."

CHAPTER VI

I

On the following day at six o'clock Ruyler went to Long's to meet Jake Spaulding. By a supreme effort of will he had put his private affairs out of his mind and concentrated on the business details which demanded the most highly trained of his faculties. But now he felt relaxed, almost languid, as he walked along Montgomery Street toward the rendezvous. He met no one he knew. The historic Montgomery Street, once the center of the city's life, was almost deserted, but half rebuilt. He could saunter and think undisturbed.

What was he to hear? And what bearing would it be found to have on his wife's conduct?

He had gone to sleep last night as sure as a man may be of anything that his wife was no more interested in Doremus than in any other of the young men who found time to dance attendance upon idle, bored, but virtuous wives.

If the man knew her secret and were endeavoring to exact blackmail he would pay his price with joy--after thrashing him, for he would have sacrificed the half of his fortune never to experience again not only the demoralizing attack of jealous madness of the night before, which had brought in its wake the uneasy doubt if civilization were as far advanced as he had fondly imagined, but the sensation of amazed contempt which had swept over him at the dinner table as he had seen his wife, whom he had believed to be a woman of instinctive taste and fastidiousness, manifestly upon intimate terms with a creature who should have been walking on four legs. Better, perhaps, the desire to kill a woman than to despise her--

He slammed the door when he entered the little room reserved for him, and barely restrained himself from flinging his hat into a corner and breaking a chair on the table. His languor had vanished.

Spaulding followed him immediately.

"Howdy," he said genially, as he pushed his own hat on the back of his head and bit hungrily at the end of a cigar. "Suppose you've been impatient--unless too busy to think about it."

"I'd like to know what you've found out as quickly as you can tell me."

"Well, to begin with the kid. I had some trouble at the convent. They're a close-mouthed lot, nuns. But I frightened them. Told them it was a property matter, and unless they answered my questions privately they'd have to answer them in court. Then they came through."

"Well?"

Spaulding lit his cigar and handed the match to Ruyler, who ground it under his heel.

"Just about nineteen years ago a Frenchwoman, giving her name as Madame Dubois, arrived one day with a child a year old and asked the nuns to take care of it, promising a fancy payment. The child had been on a farm with a wet-nurse (French style), but Madame Dubois wanted it to learn from the first to speak proper English and French, and to live in a refined atmosphere generally from the time it was able to take notice. She said she was on the stage and had to travel, so was not able to give the kid the attention it should have, and the doctor had told her that traveling was bad for kids that age, anyhow. Her lawyers would pay the baby's board on the first of every month--"

"Who were the lawyers?"

"Lawton and Cross."

"I thought so. Go on."

"The nuns, who, after all, knew their California, thought they smelt a rat, for the woman was extraordinarily handsome, magnificently dressed; the Mother Superior--who is a woman of the world, all right--read the newspapers, and had never seen the name of Dubois--and knew that only stars drew fat salaries. She asked some sharp questions about the father, and the woman replied readily that he was a scientific man, an inventor, and--well, it was natural, was it not? they did not get on very well. He disliked the stage, but she had been on it before she married him, and dullness and want of money for her own needs and her child's had driven her back. He had lived in Los Angeles for a time, but had recently gone East to take a high-salaried position. It was with his consent that she asked the nuns to take the child--possibly for two or three years. When she was a famous actress and could leave the road, she would keep house for her husband in New York, and make a home for the child.

"The Mother Superior, by this time, had made up her mind that the father wished the child removed from the mother's influence, and although she took the whole yarn with a bag of salt, the child was the most beautiful she had ever seen, and obviously healthy and amiable. Moreover, the convent was to receive two hundred dollars a month--"

"What?"

"Exactly. Can you beat it? The Mother Superior made up her mind it was her duty to bring up the little thing in the way it should go. As the woman was leaving she said something about a possible reconciliation with her family, who lived in France; they had not written her since she went on the stage. They were of a respectability!--of the old tradition! But if they came round she might take the child to them, if her husband would consent. She should like it to be brought up in France--

"Here the Mother Superior interrupted her sharply. Was her husband a Frenchman? And she answered, no doubt before she thought, for these people always forget something, that no, he was an American--her family, also, detested Americans. The Mother Superior once more interrupted her glibness. How, then, did he have a French name? Oh, but that was her stage name--she always went by it and had given it without thinking. What was her husband's name? After a second's hesitation she stupidly give the name Smith. I can see the mouth of the Mother Superior as it set in a grim line. 'Very well,' said she, 'the child's name is Helene Smith'; and although the woman made a wry face she was forced to submit.

"The child remained there four years, and the Mother Superior had some reason to believe that 'Madame Dubois' spent a good part of that time in San Francisco. She came at irregular intervals to see the child--always in vacation, when there were no pupils in the convent, and always at night. The Mother Superior, however, thought it best to make no investigations, for the child throve, they were all daffy about her, and the money came promptly on the first of every month. When the mother came she always brought a trunk full of fine underclothes, and left the money for a new uniform. Then, one day, Madame Dubois arrived in widow's weeds, said that her husband was dead, leaving her quite well off, and that she was returning to France."

"And Madame Delano's story is that he died on the way to Japan--if it is the same woman--"

"Haven't a doubt of it myself. I did a little cabling before I left last night to a man I know in Paris to find out just when Madame Delano returned with her child to live with her family in Rouen. He got busy and here is his answer--just fifteen years ago almost to the minute."

"Then who was her husband?"

"There you've got me--so far. He was no 'scientist, who later accepted a high-salaried position.' A decent chap of that sort would have written to his child, paid her board himself, most likely taken it away from the mother--"

"But she may have kidnapped it--"

"People are too easy traced in this State--especially that sort. Nor do I believe she was an actress. There never was any actress of that name--not so you'd notice it, anyhow, and that woman would have been known for her looks and height even if she couldn't act. Moreover, if she was an actress there would be no sense in giving the nuns a false name, since she had admitted the fact. No, it's my guess that she was something worse."

"Well, I've prepared myself for anything."

"I figure out that she was the mistress of one of our rich highfliers, and that when he got tired of her he pensioned her off, and she made up her mind to reform on account of the kid, and went back to Rouen, and proceeded to identify herself with her class by growing old and shapeless as quickly as possible. She must have adopted the name Delano in New York before she bought her steamer ticket, for although I've had a man on the hunt, the only Delanos of that time were eminently respectable--"

"Why are you sure she was not a--well--woman of the town?"

"Because, there again--there's no dame of that time either of that name or looks--neither Dubois nor Delano. Of course, they come and go, but there's every reason to think she stayed right on here in S.F. Of course, I've only had twenty-four hours--I'll find out in another twenty-four just what conspicuous women of fifteen to twenty years ago measure up to what she must have looked like--I got the Mother Superior to describe her minutely: nearly six feet, clear dark skin with a natural red color--no make-up; very small features, but well made--nose and mouth I'm talking about. The eyes were a good size, very black with rather thin eyelashes. Lots of black hair. Stunning figure. Rather large ears and hands and feet. She always dressed in black, the handsomest sort. They generally do."

"Well?" asked Ruyler through his teeth. He had no doubt the woman was his mother-in-law. "The Jameses? What of them?"

"That's the snag. Rest is easy in comparison. Innumerable Jameses must have died about that time, to say nothing of all the way along the line, but while some of the records were saved in 1906, most went up in smoke. Moreover, there's just the chance that he didn't die here. But that's going on the supposition that the man died when she left California, which don't fit our theory. I still think he died not so very long before her return to California, and that she probably came to collect a legacy he had left her. Otherwise, I should think it's about the last place she would have come to. I put a man on the job before I left of collecting the Jameses who've died since the fire. Here they are."

He took a list from his pocket and read:

"James Hogg, bookkeeper--races, of course. James Fowler, saloon-keeper. James Despard, called 'Frenchy,' a clever crook who lived on blackmail--said to have a gift for getting hold of secrets of men and women in high society and squeezing them good and plenty--"

He paused. "Of course, that might be the man. There are points. I'll have his life looked into, but somehow I don't believe it. I have a hunch the man was a higher-up. The sort of woman the Mother Superior described can get the best, and they take it. To proceed: James Dillingworth, lawyer, died in the odor of sanctity, but you never can tell; I'll have him investigated, too. James Maston--I haven't had time to have had the private lives of any of these men looked into, but I knew some of them, and Maston, who was a journalist, left a wife and three children and was little, if any, over thirty. James Cobham, broker--he was getting on to fifty, left about a million, came near being indicted during the Graft Prosecutions, and although his wife has been in the newspapers as a society leader for the last twenty years, and he was one of the founders of Burlingame, and then was active in changing the name of the high part to Hillsboro when the swells felt they couldn't be identified with the village any longer, and he handed out wads the first of every year to charity, there are stories that he came near being divorced by his haughty wife about fifteen years ago. Of course, those men don't parade their mistresses openly like they did thirty years ago--I mean men with any social position to keep up. But now and again the wife finds a note, or receives an anonymous letter, and gets busy. Then it's the divorce court, unless he can smooth her down, and promises reform. Cobham seems to me the likeliest man, and I'm going to start a thorough investigation to-morrow. These other Jameses don't hold out any promise at all--grocers, clerks, butchers. It's the list in hand I'll go by, and if nothing pans out--well, we'll have to take the other cue she threw out and try Los Angeles."

"Do you know anything about a man named Nicolas Doremus?" asked Ruyler abruptly.

"The society chap? Nothing much except that he don't do much business on the street but is supposed to be pretty lucky at poker and bridge. But he runs with the crowd the police can't or don't raid. I've never seen or heard of him anywhere he shouldn't be except with swell slumming or roadhouse parties. He's never interested me. If Society can stand that sort of bloodsucking tailor's model, I guess I can. Why do you ask? Got anything to do with this case?"

"I have an idea he has found out the truth and is blackmailing my wife. You might watch him."

"Good point. I will. And if he's found out the truth I guess I can."

CHAPTER VII

I

Helene, as Ruyler had anticipated, refused positively to accept Mrs. Thornton's invitation.

"Do you think I'd leave you--to come home to a dreary house every night? Even if I don't see much of you, at least you know I'm there; and that if you have an evening off you have only to say the word and I'll break any engagement--you have always known that!"

Ruyler had not, but she looked so eager and sweet--she was lunching with him at the Palace Hotel on the day following his interview with Spaulding--that he hastened to assure her affectionately that the certainty of his wife's desire for his constant companionship was both his torment and his consolation.

Helene continued radiantly:

"Besides, darling, Polly Roberts is staying on. Rex can't get away yet."

"Polly Roberts is not nearly good enough for you. She hasn't an idea in her head and lives on excitement--"

Helene laughed merrily. "You are quite right, but there's no harm in her. After all, unless one goes in for charities (and I can't, Price, yet; besides the charities here are wonderfully looked after), plays bridge, has babies, takes on suffrage--what is there to do but play? I suppose once life was serious for young women of our class; but we just get into the habit of doing nothing because there's nothing to do. Take to-morrow as an example: I suppose Polly and I will wander down to The Louvre in the morning and buy something or look at the new gowns M. Dupont has just brought from Paris.

"Then we'll lunch where there's lots of life and everybody is chatting gayly about nothing.

"Then we'll go to the Moving Pictures unless there is a matinee, and then we'll motor out to the Boulevard, and then back and have tea somewhere.

"Or, perhaps, we'll motor down to the Club at Burlingame for lunch and chatter away the day on the veranda, or dance. This afternoon we'll probably ring up a few that are still in town, and dance in Polly's parlor at the Fairmont."

Helene's lip curled, her voice had risen. With, all her young enjoyment of wealth and position, she had been bred in a class where to idle is a crime. "Just putting in time--time that ought to be as precious as youth and high spirits and ease and popularity! But what is one to do? I have no talents, and I'd lose caste in my set if I had. I don't wonder the Socialists hate us and want to put us all to work. No doubt we should be much happier. But now--even if you retired from business, you'd spend most of your time on the links. We poor women wouldn't be much better off."

"It does seem an abnormal state of affairs; I've barely given it a thought, it has always been such a pleasure to find you, after a hard day's work, looking invariably dainty, and pretty, and eloquently suggestive of leisure and repose. But--to the student of history--I suppose it is a condition that cannot last. There must be some sort of upheaval due. Well, I hope it will give me more of your society."

They smiled at each other across the little table in perfect confidence. They were lunching in the court, and after she had blown him a kiss over her glass of red wine, her eyes happened to travel in the direction of the large dining-room. She gave a little exclamation of distaste.

"There is maman lunching with that hateful old Mr. Lawton. He was in her sitting-room when I ran in to call on her yesterday, and nearly snapped my head off when I asked him if he wouldn't buy my electric for Aileen. He said it was time she began to learn a few economies instead of more extravagances. Poor darling Aileen. She has to stay in town, too, for he won't open the house in Atherton until he is ready to go down himself every night."

"Is he an old friend of your mother's?"

"She and Papa met him when they were here, and Mrs. Lawton was very kind when I was born. It's too bad Mrs. Lawton's dead. She'd be a nice friend for maman."

"Perhaps your mother is asking Mr. Lawton's advice about the investment of money."

He had been observing his wife closely, but it was more and more apparent that if Mr. Lawton held the key to her mother's past she had not been informed of the fact. She answered indifferently:

"Possibly. One can get much higher interest out here than in France, and maman would never invest money without the best advice. She loves me, but money next. Oh, la! la!"

"Has she said anything more about going back to Rouen?"

"I didn't have a word with her alone yesterday, but I'll ask her to-day. Poor maman! I fancy the novelty has worn off here, and she would really be happier with her own people and customs. She hates traveling, like all the French; but don't you think that, after a bit we shall be able to go over to Europe at least once a year?"

"I am sure of it. And while I am attending to business in London you could visit your mother in Rouen. Tell her that one way or another I'll manage it."

And this seemed to him an ideal arrangement!

II

When they left the table and walked through the more luxurious part of the court, they saw Madame Delano alone and enthroned as usual in the largest but most upright of the armchairs. And as ever she watched under her fat drooping eyelids the passing throng of smartly dressed women, hurrying men, sauntering, staring tourists. Here and there under the palms sat small groups of men, leaning forward, talking in low earnest tones, their faces, whether of the keen, narrow, nervous, or of the fleshy, heavy, square-jawed, unimaginative, aggressive, ruthless type, equally expressing that intense concentration of mind which later would make their luncheon a living torment.

Helene threw herself into a chair beside her mother and fondled her hand. Ruyler noted that after Madame Delano's surprised smile of welcome she darted a keen glance of apprehension from one to the other, and her tight little mouth relaxed uncontrollably in its supporting walls of flesh. But she lowered her lids immediately and looked approvingly at her daughter, who in her new gown of gray, with gray hat and gloves and shoes, was a dainty and refreshing picture of Spring. Then she looked at Ruyler with what he fancied was an expression of relief.

"I wonder you do not do this oftener," she said.

"I never know until the last moment when or where I shall be able to take lunch, and then I often have to meet three or four men. Such is life in the city of your adoption."

"There is no city in the world where women are so abominably idle and useless!" And at the moment, whatever Madame Delano may have been, her voice and mien were those of a virtuous and outraged bourgeoisie. "You are all very well, Ruyler, but if I had known what the life of a rich young woman was in this town, I'd have married Helene to a serious young man of her own class in Rouen; a husband who would have given her companionship in a normal civilized life, who would have taken care of her as every young wife should be taken care of, and who would have insisted upon at least two children as a matter of course. With us The Family is a religion. Here it is an incident where it is not an accident."

Ruyler, who was still standing, looked down at his mother-in-law with profound interest. He had never heard her express herself at such length before. "Do you think I fail as a husband?" he asked humbly. "God knows I'd like to give my wife about two-thirds of my time, but at least I have perfect confidence in her. I should soon cease to care for a wife I was obliged to watch."

"Young things are young things." Madame Delano looked at Helene, who had turned very white and had lowered her own lids to hide the consternation in her eyes. But as her mother ceased speaking she raised them in swift appeal to Ruyler.

"Maman says I coquette too much," she said plaintively, and Price wondered if a slight movement under the hem of Madame Delano's long skirts meant that the toe of a little gray shoe were boring into one of the massive plinths of his mother-in-law. "But tell him, maman, that you don't really mean it. I can't have Price jealous. That would be too humiliating. I'm afraid I do flirt as naturally as I breathe, but Price knows I haven't a thought for a man on earth but him." The color had crept back into her cheeks, but there was still anxiety in her soft black eyes, and Price was sure that the little pointed toe once more made its peremptory appeal.

Madame Delano looked squarely at her son-in-law.

"That's all right--so far," she said grimly. "Helene is devoted to you. But so have many other young wives been to busy American husbands. Now, take my advice, and give her more of your companionship before it is too late. **Watch over her**. There always comes a time--a turning-point--European husbands understand, but American husbands are fools. Woman's loyalty, fed on hope only, turns to resentment; and then her separate life begins. Now, I've warned you. Go back to your office, where, no doubt, your clerks are hanging out of the windows, wondering if you are dead and the business wrecked. I want to talk to Helene."

III

In spite of his wise old French mother-in-law's insinuations, Ruyler felt lighter of heart as he left the hotel and walked toward his office than he had since Sunday. Of two things he was certain: there was no ugly understanding between the mother and daughter over that unspeakable past, and Madame Delano's new attitude toward her daughter was merely the result of an over-sophisticated mother's apprehensions: those of a woman who was looking in upon smart society for the first time and found it alarming, and--unwelcome, but inevitable thought--peculiarly dangerous to a young and beautiful creature with wild and lawless blood in her veins.

However, it was patent that so far her apprehensions were merely the result of a rare imaginative flight, the result, no doubt, of her own threatened exposure. Once more he admired her courage in returning to San Francisco, and as he recalled the covert air of cynical triumph, with which she had accepted his offer for her daughter's hand, he made no doubt that one object had been to play a sardonic joke on the city she must hate.

He renewed his determination to keep what guard he could over his young wife, and wondered if his brother Harold, who also had elected to enter the old firm, could not be induced to come out and take over a certain share of the responsibility. The young man had paid him a visit a year ago and been enraptured with life in California.

True, he was accustomed to make quick decisions without consulting any one, and he should find a partner irksome, but he was beginning to realize acutely that business, even to an American brain, packed with its traditions and energies, was not even the half of life, should be a means not an end; he set his teeth as he walked rapidly along Montgomery Street and vowed that he would keep his domestic happiness if he had to retire on what was available of his own fortune. He even wondered if it would not be wise to buy a fruit ranch, where he and Helene could share equally in the management, and begin at once to raise a family. They both loved outdoor life, and this life of complete frivolity, in which she seemed to be hopelessly enmeshed, might before long corrode her nature and blast the mental aspirations that still survived in that untended soil. When this great merging deal was over he should be free to decide.

CHAPTER VIII

I

He arrived at home on the following afternoon at six and was immediately rung up by Spaulding, who demanded an interview. It was not worth while going down town again, as Helene was out and would no doubt return only in time to dress for dinner. They were to dine at half-past seven and go to the play afterward. He told Spaulding to take a taxi and come to the house.

Nothing had occurred meanwhile to cause him anxiety. He had taken Helene out to the Cliff House to dinner the night before, and afterward to see the road-houses, whose dancing is so painfully proper early in the evening. Polly Roberts had come into the most notorious of them at eleven, chaperoning a party, which included Aileen Lawton, a girl as restless and avid of excitement as herself. Rex Roberts and several other young men had been in attendance, and Polly had begged Ruyler to stay on and let his wife see something of "real life."

"This is one of the sights of the world, you know," she said, puffing her cigarette smoke into his face. "It's *too* middle-class to be shocked, and not to see occasionally what you really cannot get anywhere else. Why, there'll even be a lot of tourists here later on, and these dancers don't do the real Apache until about one. At least leave Helene with me, if you care more for bed than fun."

But Ruyler had merely laughed and taken his wife home. Helene had made no protest; on the contrary had put her arm through his in the car and her head on his shoulder, vowing she was worn out, and glad to go home. It was only afterward that it occurred to him that she had clung to him that night.

Spaulding entered the library without taking off his hat, and chewing a tooth-pick vigorously. He began to talk at once, stretching himself out in a Morris chair, and accepting a cigar. This time Price smoked with him.

"Well," said the detective, "it's like the game of button, button, who's got the button? Sometimes I think I'm getting a little warmer and then I go stone cold. But I've found out a few things, anyhow. How tall should you say Madame Delano is? I've only seen her sitting on her throne there in the Palace Court lookin' like an old Sphinx that's havin' a laugh all to herself."

"About five feet ten."

"The Mother Superior said six feet, but no doubt when she had figger instead of flesh she looked taller. Well, I've discovered no less than five tall handsome bru-nettes that sparkled here in the late Eighties and early Nineties, but it's the deuce and all to get an exact description out of anybody, especially when quite a few years have elapsed. Most people don't see details, only effects. That's what we detectives come up against all the time. So, whether these ladies were five feet eight, five feet ten, or six feet, whether they had large features or small, big hands and feet or fine points, or whether they added on all the inches they yearned for by means of high heels or style, is beyond me. But here they are."

He took his neat little note-book from his pocket and was about to read it, when Ruyler interrupted him.

"But surely you know whether these women were French or not?"

"Aw, that's just what you can't always find out. Lots of 'em pretend to be, and others--if they come from good stock in the old country--want you to forget it. But the queens generally run to French names, as havin' a better commercial value than Mary Jane or Ann Maria. One of these was Marie Garnett, who wasn't much on her own but spun the wheel in Jim's joint down on Barbary Coast, which was raided just so often for form's sake. She always made a quick getaway, was never up in court, and died young. Gabrielle ran an establishment down on Geary Street and was one of the swellest lookers and swellest togged dames in her profession till the drink got her. I can't find that she ever hooked up to a James or any one else. Pauline-Marie was another razzle-dazzle who swooped out here from nowhere and burrowed into quite a few fortunes and put quite a few of our society leaders into mourning. She disappeared and I can't trace her, but she seems to have been the handsomest of the bunch, and was fond of showing herself at first nights, dressed straight from Paris, until some of our war-hardened 'leaders' called upon the managers in a body and threatened never to set foot inside their doors again unless she was kept out, and the managers succumbed. Then there was the friend of a rich Englishman, whose first name I haven't been able to get hold of. They lived first at Santa Barbara, then loafed up and down the coast for a year or two, spending quite a time in San Francisco. She was 'foreign looking' and a stunner, all right. All of these dames drifted out about the same time--"

"What was the Englishman's name?"

"J. Horace Medford. Front name may or may not have been James. I doubt if his name could be found on any deeds, even in the south, where there was no fire. He doesn't seem to have bought any property or transacted any business. Just lived on a good-sized income. Of course, all the hotel registers here were burnt, but I wired to Santa Barbara and Monterey and got what I have given you.

"He had a yacht, and he took the woman with him everywhere. There was always a flutter when they appeared at the theater. Of course she went by his name, but as he never presented a letter all the time he was here and it was quite obvious he could have brought all he wanted, and as men are always 'on' anyhow, there was but one conclusion."

"Where did he bank? They might have his full name."

"Bank of California, but his remittances were sent to order of J. Horace Medford, and, of course, he signed his cheques the same way."

"That sounds the most likely of the lot--and the most hopeful."

"Well, haven't handed you the fifth yet, and to my mind she's the most likely of all. Ever hear of James Lawton's trouble with his wife?"

"Trouble? I thought she died."

"She--did--not. She went East suddenly about fifteen years ago, and soon after a notice of her death appeared in the San Francisco papers. But there was a tale of woe (for old Lawton) that I doubt if most of her own crowd had even a suspicion of."

"Good heavens!" Ruyler recalled the apparent intimacy of his mother-in-law and the senior member of the respectable firm of Lawton and Cross. If "Madame Delano" were the former Mrs. Lawton, how many things would be explained.

"This woman's name was Marie all right, and she was French, although she seems to have been adopted by some people named Dubois and brought up in California. She was quite the proper thing in high society, but the trouble was that she liked another sort better. She was a regular fly-by-night. It began when Norton Moore, a rotten limb of one of the grandest trees in San Francisco Society--so respectable they didn't know there was any side to life but their own--sneaked Mrs. Lawton and three girls out of his mother's house one night when she was givin' a ball, put 'em in a hack and took 'em down to Gabrielle's. There they spent an hour lookin' at Gabrielle's swell bunch dressed up and doin' the grand society act with some of the men-about-town. Then they danced some and opened a bottle or two.

"I never heard that this little jaunt hurt the girls any, but it woke up something in Mrs. Lawton. After that--well, there are stories without end. Won't take up your time tellin' them. The upshot was that one night Lawton, who took a fling himself once in a while, met her at Gabrielle's or some other joint, and she went East a day or two after. I suppose he didn't get a divorce, partly on account of the kid--Aileen--partly because he had no intention of trying his luck again."

"But is there any evidence that she had another child--that she hid away?"

"No, but it might easy have been. This life went on for about eight years, and it was at least five that she and Lawton merely lived under the same roof for the sake of Aileen. They never did get on. That much, at least, was well known. It might easy be--"

Ruyler made a rapid calculation. Aileen Lawton was just about three years older than Helene. She was fair like her father. There was no resemblance between her and his wife, but the intimacy between them had been spontaneous and had never lapsed. She had grown up quite unrestrained and spoilt, and broken three engagements, and was always rushing about proclaiming in one breath, that California was the greatest place on earth and in the next that she should go mad if she didn't get out and have a change. Another grievance was that although her father let her have her own way, or rather did not pretend to control her, he gave her a rather niggardly allowance for her personal expenses and she was supposed to be heavily in debt. Ruyler thought he could guess where a good deal of his wife's spare cash had gone to. He disliked Aileen Lawton as much as he did Polly Roberts; more, if anything, because she might have been clever and she chose to be a fool. Both of these intimate friends of his wife were the reverse of the superb outdoor type he admired.

"Good Lord!" he said. "I don't think there's much choice."

But in a moment he shook his head. "Too many things don't connect. Where did she get the money to go to her relations in Rouen--"

"He pensioned her off, of course."

"And the child? How did he consent to let her return here with a daughter he probably never had heard of--"

"I figger out, either that she came into some money from a relation over in France, or else she has something on the old boy, and wanting to come back here and marry her daughter, she held him up. He's a pillar of the church, been one of the Presidents of the Pacific-Union Club, has argued cases before the Supreme Court that have been cabled all over the country. When a man of that sort gets to Lawton's time of life he don't want any scandals."

"All the same," said Ruyler positively, "I don't believe it. I think it far more likely that he was a friend of Madame Delano's husband--assuming that she had one--and that some money was left with him in trust for her or the child."

"Well, it may be, but I incline to Lawton--"

"There's one person would know--"

"'Gene Bisbee. But I never went to that bunch yet for any information, and I don't go this time except as a last resort. Of course he knows, and that is one reason I believe she is Mrs. Lawton. He was Gabrielle's maquereau for years--when he'd wrung enough out of her he set up for himself--Well, I ain't through yet, by a long sight. Beliefs ain't proof." He rose slowly from the deep chair, stretched himself, and settled his hat firmly on his head.

"What's this I hear about a wonderful ruby your wife wore up to Gwynne's the other night? Gosh! I'd like to see a sparkler like that."

"Why, by all means."

Ruyler swung the bookcase outward, opened the safe and handed him the ruby. Spaulding regarded it with bulging eyes, and touched it with his finger tips much as he would a newborn babe. "Some stone!" he said, as he handed it back, "but why in thunder don't you keep it in a safe deposit box? There are crooks that can crack any safe, and if they got wise to this--oh, howdy, ma'am--"

Helene had come in and stood behind the two men.

Spaulding snatched off his hat and she acknowledged her husband's introduction graciously. She was dressed for the evening in white. Her eyes looked abnormally large, and she kept dropping her lids as if to keep them from setting in a stare. Her lovely mouth with its soft curves was faded and set. The whole face was almost as stiff as a mask, and even her graceful body was rigid. Ruyler saw Spaulding give her a sharp "sizing-up" look, as he murmured,

"Well, so long, Guv. See you to-morrow. Hope the man'll turn out all right after all."

"I hope so. He's a good chap otherwise."

"Good night, ma'am. Tell your husband to put that ruby in a safe deposit box."

"Oh, nobody knows the safe is there except Mr. Ruyler and myself--"

"There have been safes hidden behind bookcases before," said Spaulding dryly. "And crooks, like all the other pests of the earth, just drift naturally to this coast. If I were you I'd have a detective on hand whenever you wear that bit o' glass--not at a friendly affair like the Gwynnes' dinner, of course, but--"

"Good idea!" exclaimed Ruyler. "My wife will wear the ruby to the Thornton fete on the fourteenth. Will you be on hand to guard it?"

"Won't I? About half our force is engaged for that blow-out, but no one but yours truly shall be guardian angel for the ruby. Well, good night once more, and good luck."

*   *   *   *   *

As soon as the detective had gone Ruyler drew his wife to him anxiously, "What is it, Helene? You look--well, you don't look yourself!"

"I have a headache," she said irritably. "Perhaps I'm developing nerves. I do wish you would take me to New York. Other women get away from this town once in a while."

"But you told me on Sunday that you adored California, that it was like fairy land--"

"Oh, all the women out here bluff themselves and everybody else just so long and then suddenly go to pieces. It's a wonderful state, but what a life! What a life!

Surely I was made for something better. I don't wonder--"

"What?" he asked sharply.

"Oh, nothing. I feel ungrateful, of course. I really should be quite happy. Think if I had to go back to Rouen to live--after this taste of freedom, and beauty--for California has all the beauties of youth as well as its idiocies and vices--"

"There is not the remotest danger of your ever being obliged to live in Rouen again--"

"Oh, I don't know. You might get tired of me. We might fight like cat and dog for want of common interests, of something to talk about. You would never take to drink like so many of the men, but I might--well, I'm glad dinner is ready at last."

But she played with her food. That she was repressing an intense and mounting excitement Ruyler did not doubt, and he also suspected that she wished to broach some particular subject from which she turned in panic. They were alone after coffee had been served, and he said abruptly:

"What is it, Helene? Do you want money? I have an idea that Polly Roberts and Aileen Lawton borrow heavily from you, and that they may have cleaned you out completely on the first--"

"How dear of you to guess--or rather to get so close. It's worse than that. I--that is--well--poor Polly went quite mad over a pearl necklace at Shreve's and they told her to take it and wear it for a few days, thinking, I suppose, she would never give it up and would get the money somehow. She--oh, it's too dreadful--she lost it--and she dares not tell Rex--he's lost quite a lot of money lately--and she's mad with fright--and I told her--"

"Where did she lose it? It's not easy to lose a necklace, especially when the clasp is new."

"She thinks it was stolen from her neck at the theater--you heard what that man said."

"Ah! What was the price of the necklace?"

"Twenty thousand dollars. The pearls weren't so very large, of course, but Polly never had had a pearl necklace--"

"I'll let her have the money to pay for it on one condition--that it is a transaction, between Roberts and myself--"

"No! No! Not for anything!"

"I've lent him money before--"

"But he'd never forgive Polly. He--he's one of those men who make an awful fuss on the first of every month when his wife's bills come in."

"There must be a bass chorus on the first of every month in San Francisco--"

"Oh, please don't jest. She must have this money."

"She may have it--on those terms. I'll have no business dealings with women of the Polly Roberts sort. That would be the last I'd ever see of the twenty thousand--"

"I never thought you were stingy!"

Ruyler, in spite of his tearing anxiety, laughed outright. "Is that your idea of how the indulgent American husband becomes rich?"

"Oh--of course I wouldn't have you lose such a sum. I really have learned the value of money in the abstract, although I can't care for it as much as men do."

"I have no great love of money, but there is a certain difference between a miser and a levelheaded business man--"

"Price, I must have that money. Polly--oh, I am afraid she will kill herself!"

"Not she. A more selfish little beast never breathed. She'll squeeze the money out of some one, never fear! But I think I'll lock up your jewels in case you are tempted to raise money on them for her--Darling!"

Helene, without a sound, had fainted.

CHAPTER IX

They had intended to go to the theater but Ruyler put her to bed at once. He offered to read to her, but she turned her back on him with cold disdain, and he went to the little invisible cupboard where she kept her own jewels and took out the heavy gold box which had been the wedding present of one of his California business friends who owned a quartz mine.

"I shall put this in the safe," he said incisively, "for, while I admire your stanchness in friendship, even for such an unworthy object as Polly Roberts, I do not propose that my wife shall be selling or pawning her jewels for any reason whatever. Think over the proposal I made downstairs. If Polly is willing I'll lend Roberts the money to-morrow."

She had thrown an arm over her face and she made no reply. He went down stairs and put the box in the safe. It occurred to him that she had watched him open and close the safe several times but she certainly never had written the combination down, and it had taken him a long while to commit it to memory himself.

He had glanced over the contents of the box before he locked it in. The jewels were all there, the string of pearls that he had given her on their marriage day, a few wedding presents, and several rings and trinkets he had bought for her since. The value was perhaps twenty thousand dollars, for he had told her that she must wait several years before he could give her the jewels of a great lady. When she was thirty, and really needed them to make up for fading charms--it had been one of their pleasant little jokes.

As Ruyler set the combination he sighed and wondered whether their days of joking were over. Their life had suddenly shot out of focus and it would require all his ingenuity and patience, aided by friendly circumstance, to swing it into line again. He did not believe a word of the necklace story. Somebody was blackmailing the poor child. If he could only find out who! He made up his mind suddenly to put this problem also in the hands of Spaulding for solution. The question of his mother-in-law's antecedents was important enough, but that of his wife's happiness and his own was paramount.

He decided to go to the theater himself, for he was in no condition for sleep or the society of men at the club, nor could any book hold his attention. He prayed that the play would be reasonably diverting.

He walked down town and as he entered the lobby of the Columbia at the close of the first act he saw 'Gene Bisbee and D.V. Bimmer, who was now managing a hotel in San Francisco, standing together. He also saw Bisbee nudge Bimmer, and they both stared at him openly, the famous hotel man with some sympathy in his wise secretive eyes, the reformed peer of the underworld with a certain speculative contempt.

Ruyler, to his intense irritation, felt himself flushing, and wondered if the man's regard might be translated: "Just how much shall I be able to touch him for?" He wished he would show his hand and dissipate the damnable web of mystery which Fate seemed weaving hourly out of her bloated pouch, but he doubted if Bisbee, or whoever it was that tormented his wife, would approach him save as a last resource. They were clever enough to know that her keenest desire would be to keep the disgraceful past from the knowledge of her husband, rather than from a society seasoned these many years to erubescent pasts.

Moreover it is always easier to blackmail a woman than a man, and Price Ruyler could not have looked an easy mark to the most optimistic of social brigands.

He found it impossible to fix his mind on the play; the cues of the first act eluded him, and the characters and dialogue were too commonplace to make the story negligible.

At the end of the second act Ruyler made up his mind to go home and try to coax his wife back into her customary good temper, pet her and make her forget her little tragedy. He still hesitated to broach the subject to her directly, but it was possible that by some diplomatically analogous tale he could surprise her into telling him the truth.

During the long drive he turned over in his mind the data Spaulding had placed before him during the afternoon. He rejected the theory that Madame Delano was

Mrs. Lawton as utterly fantastic, but admitted a connection. Helene had spoken more than once of Mrs. Lawton's kindness to "maman" when her baby was born during her "enforced stay in San Francisco," and it was quite possible that the two had been friends, and that the young mother had adopted the name of Dubois when calling upon the nuns of the convent at St. Peter, either because it would naturally occur to her, or from some deeper design which, he could not fathom....

Yes, the connection with Mrs. Lawton was indisputable and it remained for him to "figger out" as Spaulding would say, which of these women, the gambler's wife, the notorious "Madam," Gabrielle, the briefly coruscating Pauline Marie, or the Englishman's mistress, a woman of Mrs. Lawton's position would be most likely to befriend.

The first three might be dismissed without argument. She had been no frequenter of "gambling joints" whatever her peccadilloes; Gabrielle, he happened to know, had died some eight or ten years ago, and Mademoiselle Pauline Marie, if she had had a child, which was extremely doubtful, was the sort that sends unwelcome offspring post haste to the foundling asylum.

There remained only the spurious Mrs. Medford, and she was the probability on all counts. What more likely than that she and Mrs. Lawton had met at one of the great winter hotels in Southern California, and foregathered? Certainly they would be congenial spirits.

When the baby came Mrs. Lawton would naturally see her through her trouble, and advise her later what to do with the child. No doubt, Medford found it in the way.

After that Ruyler could only fumble. Did Medford desert the woman, driving her on the stage?--or elsewhere? Did they start for Japan, and did he die on the voyage? Did he merely give the woman a pension and tell her to go back to Rouen, or to the devil? It was positive that when Helene was five years old Madame Delano had gone back to her relatives with some trumped up story and been received by them.

Moreover, this theory coincided with, his belief that Helene's father was a gentleman. No doubt he had been already married when he met the young French girl, superbly handsome, and intelligent--possibly at one of the French watering places, even in Rouen itself, swarming with tourists in Summer. They might have met in the spacious aisles of the Cathedral, she risen from her prayers, he wandering about, Baedeker in hand, and fallen in love at sight. One of Earth's million romances, regenerating the aged planet for a moment, only to sink back and disappear into her forgotten dust.

His own romance? What was to be the end of that!

But he returned to his argument. He wanted a coherent story to tell his wife, and he wanted also to believe that his wife's father had been a gentleman.

Medford, like so many of his eloping kind, had made instinctively for California with the beautiful woman he loved but could not marry. Santa Barbara, Ruyler had heard, had been the favorite haven for two generations of couples fleeing from irking bonds in the societies of England and the continent of Europe. Southern California combined a wild independence with a languor that blunted too sensitive nerves, offered an equable climate with months on end of out of door life, boating, shooting, riding, driving, motoring, romantic excursions, and even sport if a distinguished looking couple played the game well and told a plausible story.

Breeding was a part of Ruyler's religion, as component in his code as honor, patriotism, loyalty, or the obligation of the strong to protect the weak. Far better the bend sinister in his own class than a legitimate parent of the type of 'Gene Bisbee or D.V. Bimmer. Ruyler was a "good mixer" when business required that particular form of diplomacy, and the familiarities of Jake Spaulding left his nerves unscathed, but in bone and brain cells he was of the intensely respectable aristocracy of Manhattan Island and he never forgot it. He had surrendered to a girl of no position without a struggle, and made her his wife, but it is doubtful if he would even have fallen in love with her if she had been underbred in appearance or manner. He had never regretted his marriage for a moment, not even since this avalanche of mystery and portending scandal had descended upon him; if possible he loved his troubled young wife more than ever--with a sudden instinct that worse was to come he vowed that nothing should ever make him love her less.

When he arrived at his house he found two notes on the hall table addressed to himself. The first was from Helene and read:

"Polly telephoned that she would send her car for me to go down to the Fairmont and dance. I cannot sleep so I am going. *She cannot sleep either*! Forgive me if I was cross, but I am terribly worried for her. Don't wait up for me. Helene."

He read this note with a frown but without surprise. It was to be expected that she would seek excitement until her present fears were allayed and her persecutors silenced.

He determined to order Spaulding to have her shadowed constantly for at least a fortnight and note made of every person in whose company she appeared to be at all uneasy, whether they were of her own set or not. It would also be worth while to have Madame Delano's rooms watched, for it was possible that she would summon Helene there to meet Bisbee or others of his ilk.

Then he picked up the other note. It was from Spaulding, and as he read it all his finespun theories vanished and once more he was adrift on an uncharted sea without a landmark in sight.

"Dear Sir," began the detective, who was always formal on paper. "I've just got the information required from Holbrook Centre. We didn't half believe there was such a place, if you remember? Well there is, and according to the parish register Marie Jeanne Perrin was married to James Delano on July 25th, 1891. She was there, visiting some French relations--they went back soon after--and he had left there when he was about sixteen and had only come back that once to see his mother, who was dying. Nothing seems to have been known about him in his home town except a sort of rumor that he was a bad lot and lived somewheres in California. Can you beat it? But don't think I'm stumped. I'm working on a new line and I'm not going to say another word until I've got somewheres.

"Yours truly,

"J. SPAULDING."

"Delano's father was a Forty-niner, and lived in California till 1860, when he went home to H. C. and died soon after. There were wild stories about him, too."

CHAPTER X

I

During the next few days Ruyler saw little of his wife. He was obliged to take two business trips out of town and as he could not return until ten o'clock at night he advised her to have company to dinner and take her guests to the play. But she preferred to dine with Polly Roberts and Aileen Lawton, and she spent her days for the most part at Burlingame, motoring down with one or more of her friends, or sent for by some enthusiastic girl admirer already established there for the summer.

Ruyler was quite willing to forego temporarily his plan of personal guardianship, as the more she roamed abroad unattended the better could Spaulding watch her associates. The detective had his agents in society, as well as in the Palace Hotel, and on the third day he sent a brief note to Ruyler announcing that he had "lit on to something" that would make his employer's "hair curl, but no more at present from yours truly."

"This time," he added, "I'm on the right track and know it. No more fancy theories. But I won't say a word till I can deliver the goods. Give your wife all the rope you can."

Price and Helene met briefly and amiably and she did not again broach the subject of the loan for her friend, nor did she ask for her jewels. It was apparent that she was proudly determined to conceal whatever terrors or even worries that might haunt her, but the effort deprived her of all her native vivacity; she was almost formal in manner and her white face grew more like a classic mask daily.

On the evening before the Thornton fete, however, Price was able to dine at home. They met at table and he saw at once that she either had recovered her spirits or was making a deliberate attempt to create the impression of a carefree young woman happy in a tete-a-tete dinner with a busy husband.

Her talk for the most part was of the great entertainment at San Mateo. The weather promised to be simply magnificent. Wasn't that exactly like Flora Thornton's luck? The immense grounds were simply swarming with workmen; wagon-loads of all sorts of things went through the gates after every train--simply one procession after another; but no one else could so much as get her nose through those gates.

Helene, with all her old childish glee, related how she and Aileen, Polly (who apparently had forgotten her impending doom), and two or three other girls, had called up Mrs. Thornton on the telephone every ten minutes for an hour--pretending it was long distance to make sure of a personal response--and begged to be allowed to go over and see the preparations, until finally, in a towering rage, her ladyship had replied that if they called her again she would withdraw her invitations.

"How we did long for an airship. It would have been such fun, for she does so disapprove of all of us; thinks us a little flock of silly geese. Well, we are, I guess, but wasn't she one herself once? She has a pretty hard time even now making life interesting for herself--out here, anyhow.

"Yesterday we motored down to Menlo and dropped in at the Maynards. There were a lot of the props of San Francisco society, all as rich as croesus, sitting on the veranda crocheting socks or sacks for a crop of new babies that are due. One or two were hemstitching lawn, or embroidering a monogram, or something else equally useless or virtuous. They were talking mild gossip, and didn't even have powder on. It was ghastly--"

"Helene," said Ruyler abruptly, "what do you think is the secret of happiness--I mean, of course, the enduring sort--perhaps content would be the better word. Happiness is too dependent upon love, and love was never meant for daily food. You are not by nature frivolous, and you are capable of thought. Have you ever given any to the secret of content?"

"Yes, work," she answered promptly. "Everybody should have his daily job, prescribed either by the state or by necessity; but something he must do if both he and society would continue to exist."

Ruyler elevated his eyebrows and looked at her curiously. "Socialism. I didn't know you had ever heard of it."

"Aileen and I are not such fools as we look--as you were good enough to intimate just now. We went to a series of lectures early last winter over at the University, on Socialism--a lot of us formed a class, but all except Aileen and I dropped out.

"We continued to read for a time after the lectures were over, but of course that didn't last. One drops everything for want of stimulus, and when one begins to flutter again one is lost.

"But I heard and read and thought enough to deduce that the only vital interest in life after one's secret happiness--which one would not dare spread out too thin if one could in this American life--is necessary work well done. And that is quite different from those fussy interests and fads we create or take up for the sake of thinking we are busy and interested.

"Polly's mother once told me she never was so happy in her life as during those weeks after the earthquake and fire when all the servants had run away and she had to cook for the family out in the street on a stove they bought down in a little shop in Polk Street and set up and surrounded on three sides by 'inside blinds.' She happened to have a talent for cooking, and without her the family would have starved. Polly tied a towel round her head and did the housework, or stood in a line and got the daily rations from the Government. She never thought once of--"

"Of what?"

"Oh, of doing anything rather than expire of boredom. She and Rex had been married a year and were living at home. Rex and Mr. Carter helped excavate down in the business district, as the working class wouldn't lift a finger as long as the Government was feeding them."

"There you are! Their ideal is complete leisure, and that of our delicate products of the highest civilization--compulsory jobs! What does progress mean but the leisure to enjoy the arts and all the finer fruits of progress? What else do we men really work for?"

"Progress has gone too far and defeated its own ends. Every healthy human being should be forced to work six hours a day.

"That would leave eight for sleep and ten for enjoyment of the arts and luxuries. Then we really should enjoy them, and if we couldn't have them unless we did our six hours' stint, ennui and the dissipations that it breeds would be unknown.

"I can tell you it is demoralizing, disintegrating, to wake up morning after morning--about ten o'clock!--and know that you have nothing worth while to do for another day--for all the days!--that you have no place in the world except as an ornament! Women of limited incomes and a family of growing children have enough, to do, of course--too much--they never can feel superfluous and demoralized--except by envy--but as for us! Why, I can tell you, it is a marvel we don't all go straight to the devil."

They were alone with the coffee, and she was pounding the table with her little fist. Her cheeks were deeply flushed and her black somber eyes were opening and closing rapidly, as if alternately magnetized by some ugly vision and sweeping it aside.

Price watched her with deep interest and deeper anxiety. "A good many women go to the devil," he said. "But you are not that sort."

"Oh, I don't know. I never could get up enough interest in another man to solve the problem in the usual way--but there are other resources--I--well--"

"What?" Price sat up very straight.

"Oh, dance ourselves into tuberculosis," she said lightly, and dropping her eyelashes. "And tuberculosis of the mind, certainly. On the whole, I think I prefer physical to spiritual death....

"However--I found out one thing to-day. The dancing is to be out of doors. There will be an immense arbor or something of the sort erected on the lawn above the sunken garden. My gown is a dream and I shall wear the ruby."

"Yes," he said smiling. "You shall wear the ruby. But you must expect me to keep very close to you--"

"The closer the better." She smiled charmingly. "Have you tried on your costume?"

"I haven't even looked at it. Who am I?"

"Caesar Borgia. You are not much like him yourself, darling, but I thought he was not so very unlike modern American business, as a whole."

Ruyler laughed. "Why not Machiavelli? But as no doubt it is black velvet, much puffed and slashed, I may hope it will be becoming to my nondescript fairness. You must promise not to wander off for long walks with any of your admirers. Not that I fear the admirers, but the thieves that are bound to get into that crowd one way or another. They have a way of unclasping necklaces even of the most circumspect wives in the company of not too absorbing men."

Her eyes opened and flashed, but he had no time to analyze that fleeting expression before she was promising volubly not to wander from the illuminated spaces.

*   *   *   *   *

He interrupted her suddenly. They were in the library now, and sat down on a little sofa in front of the window. The moon was high and brilliant and the great expanse of water with the high clusters of lights on the islands, the sharp hard silhouette of the encircling mountains, the green and silver stars so high above, the moving golden dots of an incoming liner from Japan, the long rows of arc lights along the shore, made a landscape of the night that Mrs. Thornton with all her millions hardly could rival.

"Are you not grateful for this?" he asked whimsically and a little wistfully.

"Oh, Price, dear, I am more grateful than you will ever know. I have not a fault on earth to find with you. You would be the prince of the fairy tale if you were not so busy.

"But that is the tragedy. You are busy--I am not."

"Well, let us have the personal solution--one that fits ourselves. You have time to think it out. I, alas! have not." He took her hand and fondled it, hoping for her confidence.

"I don't know." She had a deep rich voice and she could make it very intense. "I only know there must--must--be a change--if--if--I am to--Can't you take me abroad for a year? That might not be work, but at least I should be learning some thing--I have traveled almost not at all--and, at least, I should have you."

"But later? Most of your friends have spent a good deal of time in Europe. I doubt if any state in the Union goes to Europe as often as California! They are all the more discontented when they come back here to vegetate--as Mrs. Thornton would express it.

"It would be a blessed interval, but no more."

"We should have time to think out a new and different life....

"You know--in the class I come from--in France--the women are the partners of their husbands. Even in the higher bourgeoisie, that is, where they still are in business, not living on great inherited fortunes--

"My uncle had a small silk house in Rouen, and my aunt kept the books and attended to all the correspondence. He always said she was the cleverer business man of the two; but French women have a real genius for business. Some of our great ladies help their husbands manage their estates.

"It is only the few that live for pleasure and glitter in the most glittering city in the world that have furnished the novelists the material to give the world a false impression of France.

"The majority live such sober, useful, busy lives that only the highest genius could make people read about them.

"Of course, young girls dream of something far more brilliant, and wait eagerly for the husband who shall deliver them from their narrow restricted little spheres... perhaps take them to the great world of Paris; but they settle down, even in Paris, and devote themselves to their husbands' interests, which are their own, and to their children....

"That is it! They are indispensable--not as women, but as partners. I barely know what your business is about--only that you are in some tremendous wholesale commission thing with tentacles that reach half round the world.

"Only the wives of politicians are any real help to their husbands in this country. Isabel Gwynne! What a help she will be--has been--to Mr. Gwynne. But then she was always busy. When her uncle died he left her that little ranch and scarcely anything else, she took to raising chickens--not to fuss about and fill in her time, but to keep a roof over her head and have enough to eat and wear. I doubt if she ever was bored in her life."

"I can't take you into the business, sweetheart," said Ruyler slowly. "For that would violate the traditions of a very old conservative house. But I can quite see that something must be done....

"I married you to make you happy and to be happy myself. I do not intend that our marriage shall be a failure. It is possible that Harold would consent to come out here and take my place. The business no longer requires any great amount of initiative, but the most unremitting vigilance. I have thought--it has merely passed through my mind--but you might hate it--how would you like it if I bought a large fruit ranch, several thousand acres, and put up a canning factory besides? I would make you a full partner and you would have to give to your share of the work considerably more than six hours of the day--

"We could build a large, plain, comfortable house, take all our books and pictures, subscribe to all the newspapers, magazines and reviews, keep up with everything that is going on in the world, have house parties once in a while, come to town for a few weeks in summer for the plays.

"We should live practically an out-of-door life--if you preferred we could buy a cattle ranch in the south. That would mean the greater part of the day in the saddle--

"How does it appeal to you?"

He had turned off the electricity, but as he fumbled with his embryonic idea he saw her eyes sparkle and a light of passionate hope dawn on her face.

"Oh, I should love it! But love it! Especially the fruit ranch. That would be like France--our orchards are as wonderful as yours, even if nothing could be as big as a California ranch--

"That is, if it would not be a makeshift. Another form of playing at life."

"I can assure you that we will have to make it pay or go to the wall. My father would probably disinherit me, for it would be breaking another tradition, and he compliments me by believing that I am the best business man in the firm at present.

"My only capital would be such of my fortune as is not tied up in the House--about a hundred thousand dollars in Government bonds. Of course, in time, if all goes well, and California does not have another setback--if business improves all over the world--I shall be able to take the rest of my money out, that I put into this end of the business after the fire; but that may be ten years hence. I shouldn't even ask for interest on it--that would be the only compensation I could offer for deserting the firm.

"Perhaps I had better buy a cattle ranch. Then, if we fail, I shall at least have had the training of a cowboy and can hire out."

Helene laughed and clapped her hands.

"Fail? You? But I should help you to make it a success--I should be really necessary?"

"Indispensable. Either you or another partner."

"No! No! I shall be the partner--"

"And you mean that you would be willing to bury your youth, your beauty, on a ranch? I have heard bitter confidences out here from women forced to waste their youth on a ranch. You are one of the fine flowers of civilization--"

"That soon wither in the hothouse atmosphere. I wish to become a hardy annual. And when the ranch was running like a clock we could take a month or two in Europe every year or so--"

"Rather! And I could show you off--Bother! I'll not answer."

The telephone bell on the little table in the corner (his own private wire) rang so insistently that Ruyler finally was magnetized reluctantly across the room. He put the receiver to his ear and asked, "Well?" in his most inhospitable tones.

The answer came in Spaulding's voice, and in a moment he sat down.

At the end of ten minutes he hung the receiver on the hook and returned to find Helene standing by the window, all the light gone from her eyes, staring out at the hard brilliant scene with an expression of hopelessness that had relaxed the very muscles of her face.

Ruyler was shocked, and more apprehensive than he had yet been. "Helene!" he exclaimed. "What is the matter? Surely you may confide in me if you are in trouble."

"Oh, but I am not," she replied coldly. "Did I look odd? I was just wondering how many really happy people there were behind those lights--over on Belvedere, at Sausalito--the lights look so golden and steady and sure--and glimpses of interiors at night are always so fascinating--but I suppose most of the people are commonplace and just dully discontented--"

"Well, I am afraid I have something to tell you that hardly will restore your delightful gayety of a few moments ago. I am sorry--but--well, the fact is I must leave for the north to-morrow morning and hardly shall be able to return before the next night. I am really distressed. I wanted so much to take you to-morrow night--"

"And I can't wear the ruby?" Her voice was shrill. Ruyler wondered if his stimulated imagination fancied a note of terror in it.

"I--I--am afraid not--darling--"

"But that Spaulding man will be there to watch--"

"Unfortunately--I forgot to tell you--he cannot go--he is on an important case. Besides--when I make a promise I usually keep it."

"But--but--" She stammered as if her brain were confused, then turned and pressed her face to the window. "I suppose nothing matters," she said dully. "Perhaps you will let me wear my own little ruby. After all, that was maman's, and she gave it to me before I was married. I should like to wear one jewel."

"You shall have all your jewels, if you will promise not to give them to Polly Roberts or any one else."

"I promise."

He went over and opened the safe, and when he rose with the gold jewel case he saw that she was standing behind him. Once more it flitted through his mind that she had watched him manipulate the combination several times, but he had little confidence in any but a professional thief's ability to memorize such an involved assortment of figures as had been invented for this particular safe. It was only once in a while that he was not obliged to refer to the key that he carried in his pocketbook.

Nor was she looking at the safe, but staring upward at a maharajah, covered with pearls of fantastic size. She took the box from his hand with a polite word of thanks, offered her cheek to be kissed, and left the room.

Price threw himself into a chair and rehearsed the instructions Spaulding had given him.

CHAPTER XI

It was half-past eleven when Ruyler and Spaulding, masked and wearing colored silk dominoes, entered the great gates of the Thornton estate in San Mateo, the detective merely displaying something in his palm to the stern guardians that kept the county rabble at bay.

The mob stood off rather grumblingly, for they would have liked to get closer to that gorgeous mass of light they could merely glimpse through the great oaks of the lower part of the estate, and to the music so seductive in the distance.

They were not a rabble to excite pity, by any means. A few ragged tramps had joined the crowd, possibly a few pickpockets from the city, watching their opportunity to slip in behind one of the automobiles that brought the guests from the station or from the estates up and down the valley. They were, for the most part, trades-people from the little towns--San Mateo, Redwood City--or the wives of the proletariat--or the servants of the neighboring estates. But, although, they grumbled and envied, they made no attempt to force their way in; it was only the light-fingered gentry the police at the great iron gates were on the lookout for.

Ruyler, if his mind had been less harrowed with the looming and possibly dire climax of his own secret drama, would have laughed aloud at this melodramatic entrance to the grounds of one of his most intimate friends. He and Spaulding had walked from the train, but they were not detained as long as a gay party of young people from Atherton, who teased the police by refusing to present their cards or lift their masks. Ruyler knew them all, but they finally sped past him without even a glance of contempt for mere foot passengers, even though they looked like a couple of dodging conspirators.

He had met Spaulding at the station in San Francisco, and private conversation on the crowded train had been impossible. When they had walked a few yards along the wide avenue, as brilliant as day with its thousands of colored lights concealed in the astonished pines, Ruyler sat deliberately down upon a bench and motioned the detective to take the seat beside him.

"It is time you gave me some sort of a hint," he said. "After all, it is my affair--"

"I know, but as I said, you might not approve my methods, and if you balk, all is up. We've got the chance of our lives. It's now or never."

"I do not at all like the idea that you may be forcing me into a position where I may find myself doing something I shall be ashamed of for the rest of my life."

Ruyler's tone was haughty. He did not relish being led round by the nose, and his nerves were jumping.

"Now! Now!" said Spaulding soothingly, as he lit a cigar. "When you hire a detective you hire him to do things you wouldn't do yourself; and if you won't give him the little help he's got to have from you or quit, what's the use of hiring him at all?

"I know perfectly well that nothing but your own eyes would convince you of what it's up to me to prove--to say nothing of the fact that I count on your entrance at the last minute to put an end to the whole bad business. For it is a bad business--believe me. But not a word of that now. You couldn't pry open my lips with a five dollar Havana."

"Well--you say you had a talk with Madame Delano to-day. Surely you can tell me some of the things you have discovered."

"A whole lot. I've been waiting for the chance. Not that I got anything out of her. She's one grand bluffer and no mistake. I take off my hat to her. When I told her that I could lay hands on the proof that she was Marie Garnett--although Jim had married her in his home town under his own name--and that she'd gone home to France with the kid when it was five, taking the cue from her friend, Mrs. Lawton, and sending word back she was dead--"

"You were equally sure a few days ago that she was Mrs. Lawton--"

"That was just my constructive imagination on the loose. It was a lovely theory, and I sort of hung on to it. But I had no real data to go on. Now I've got the evidence that Jim Garnett died two months before the fire burnt up pretty nearly all the records, and that his body was shipped back to Holbrook Centre to be buried in the family plot. You see, he was sick for some time out on Pacific Avenue, and his death was registered where the fire didn't go--"

"But what put you on?" asked Ruyler impatiently. "I should almost rather it had been any one else. He seems to have been about as bad a lot as even this town ever turned out."

"He was, all right, and his father before him, although they came from mighty fine folks back east. His father came out in '49 with the gold rush crowd, panned out a good pile, and then, liking the life--San Francisco was a gay little burg those days--opened one of the crack gambling houses down on the Old Plaza. Plate glass windows you could look through from outside if you thought it best to stay out, and see hundreds of men playing at tables where the gold pieces--often slugs--were piled as high as their noses, and hundreds more walking up and down the aisles either waiting for a chance to sit, or hoping to appease their hunger with the sight of so much gold. They didn't try any funny business, for every gambler had a six-shooter in his hip pocket, and sometimes on the table beside him.

"Sometimes men would walk out and shoot themselves on the sidewalk in front of the windows, and not a soul inside would so much as look up. Well, Delano the first had a short life but a merry one. He couldn't keep away from the tables himself, and first thing he knew he was broke, sold up. He went back to the mines, but his luck had gone, and his wife--she had followed him out here--persuaded him to go back home and live in the old house, on a little income she had; and he bored all the neighbors to death for a few years about 'early days in California' until he dropped off. Her name was Mary Garnett.

"That's what put me on--the G. in the middle of the name of the man Madame Delano married. I telegraphed to Holbrook Centre to find out what his middle name was, and after that it was easy. I also found out that he was born in California, and I guess that old wild life was in his blood. He stood Holbrook Centre until he was sixteen, and then homed back and took up the trade he just naturally had inherited.

"I figger out that he didn't tell his wife the truth when he married her back there, not until he was on the train pretty close to S.F., and then he told her because he couldn't help himself. She couldn't help herself, either, and besides she was in love with him. He was a handsome, distinguished lookin' chap, and he kept right on bein' a fascinator as long as he lived.

"I guess that's the reason she left him in the end. She stood for the gambling joint, and, although she had a cool sarcastic way with her that kept the men who fell for her at a distance, she was a good decoy, and she looked a regular queen at the head of the green table. She was chummy with Jim's intimates, two of whom were D.V. Bimmer and 'Gene Bisbee, but even 'Gene didn't dare take any liberties with her.

"It was natural that a woman brought up as she had been should have kept her child out of it, and I figger that she got disgusted with Jim and came to the full sense of her duty to the poor kid about the same time. But she didn't go until Jim settled so much a month on her through old Lawton--who used to amuse himself at Garnett's a good deal in those days, and who was one of her best friends.

"Well, she also got Garnett to make a curious sort of a will, leaving his money to James Lawton, to 'dispose of as agreed upon.' She had a thrifty business head, had that French dame, and she had made him buy property when he was flush, and put it in her name, although she gave a written agreement never to sell out as long as he lived.

"He agreed to let her go because he was dippy about another skirt at the time, and, besides, she played on his family pride--lineal descendant of the Delanos, Garnetts, and so forth. He'd never seen the kid after it was taken to the convent, but I guess he liked the idea, all right, of its being brought up wearing the old name, and gettin' rid of Marie at the same time.

"She was too canny to leave him a loophole for divorce, even in California; but I guess that didn't worry him much.

"If the earthquake and fire hadn't come so soon after the will was probated there might have been a lot of speculation about it, among men, at least. Those old gossips in the Club windows would soon have been putting two and two together; but the calamity that burnt up all the Club windows, just swept it clean out of their heads.

"I figger out that old Lawton continued to pay Madame Delano the income she'd been havin' both from Jim and her properties, out of his own pocket, until the city was rebuilt and he could settle the estate. He had to borrow the money to rebuild the houses Jim had put up on his wife's property, and when things got to a certain pass he wrote Madame D. to come along and take over her property. She'll be good and rich one of these days, when all the mortgages are paid off and Lawton paid back, but it was wise for her to stay on the job. Lawton is dead straight, but his partner is sowing wild oats in his old age--good old S.F. style, and I guess it ain't wise to tempt him too far. Get me?"

"It's atrocious!"

"Oh, not nearly so bad as it might be. Just think, if it had been Gabrielle, or Pauline-Marie, or even Mrs. Lawton. That's the worst kind of bad blood for a woman to inherit. Marie Garnett hung on like grim death to what the grand society you move in pretends to value most, and the Lord knows she'll never lose it now.

"Nor need there be any scandal to drive your family to suicide. The thing to do is to hustle Madame Delano out of San Francisco. She'll go, all right, with you to look after her interests. She don't fancy being recognized and blackmailed, or I miss my guess. You may have to pay Bisbee something, but D. V.'s not that sort, and I don't think anybody else is on. If they've suspected they'll soon forget it when the old lady disappears from the Palace Hotel. Gee, but she has a nerve."

"She is an old cynic. If she had any snobbery in her she'd be here to-night, rubbing elbows with the women who never knew of her existence twenty years ago, although their husbands did. It has satisfied her ironic French soul to sit in the court of the Palace Hotel day after day and defy San Francisco to recognize Marie Garnett in the obese Madame Delano, whose daughter is one of the great ladies of the city to whose underworld she once belonged, and from whose filthy profits she derives her income. Good God!"

He sat forward and clutched his head, but Spaulding, who had drawn out his watch, tapped him on the shoulder.

"Come on," he said. "Time's gettin' short. The stunt is to be pulled off just before supper."

CHAPTER XII

I

They walked rapidly up the close avenue--planted far back in the Fifties by Ford Thornton's grandfather--the blaze of light at the end of the long perspective growing wider and wider. As they emerged they paused for a moment, dazzled by the scene.

The original home of the Thorntons had been of ordinary American architecture and covered with ivy; it might have been transplanted from some old aristocratic village in the East. Flora Thornton had maintained that only one style of architecture was appropriate in a state settled by the Spaniards, and famous for its missions of Moorish architecture. Fordy loved the old house, but as he denied his wife nothing he had given her a million, three years before the fire which so sadly diminished fortunes, and told her to build any sort of house she pleased; if she would only promise to live in it and not desert him twice a year for Europe.

The immense structure, standing on a knoll, bore a certain resemblance to the Alhambra, with its heavy square towers; its arched gateways leading into courtyards with fountains or sunken pools, the red brown of the stucco which looked like stone and was not. To-night it was blazing with lights of every color.

So were the ancient oaks, which were old when the Alhambra was built, the shrubberies, the vast rose garden. The surface of the pool in the sunken garden reflected the green or red masses of light that shot up every few moments from the four corners of the terrace surrounding it. On the lawn just above and to the right of the house, a platform had been built for dancing; it was enclosed on three sides with an arbor of many alcoves, lined with flowers, soft lights concealed in depending clusters of oranges.

And everywhere there were people dressed in costumes, gorgeous, pictur-esque, impressive, historic, or recklessly invented, but suggesting every era when dress counted at all. They danced on the great platform to the strains of the invisible band, strolled along the terraces above the sunken garden, wandered through the groves and "grounds," or sat in the windows of the great house or in its courts. All wore the little black satin mask prescribed by Mrs. Thornton, and created an illu-sion that transported the imagination far from California. Ruyler had a whimsical sense of being on another star where the favored of the different periods of Earth had foregathered for the night.

But there was nothing ghostly in the shrill chatter as incessant as the twitter of the agitated birds, who found their night snatched from them and hardly knew whether to scold or join in the chorus.

Ruyler had always protested against the high-pitched din made by even six American women when gathered together, and to the infernal racket at any large entertainment; but to-night he sighed, forgetting his apprehensions for the mo-ment.

He had exquisite memories of these lovely grounds; he and Helene had spent several days with Mrs. Thornton during their engagement, and she had lent them the house for their honeymoon; he would have liked to wander through the pleas-ant spaces with his wife to-night and make love to her, instead of spying on her in the company of a detective.

For that, he was forced to conclude, was what he had been brought for. Spauld-ing had mentioned her name casually, when telling him that he must be on hand to nab the "party" who was at the bottom of the whole trouble; but Spaulding hardly could have watched the person who was blackmailing without including her in his surveillance. He wished now that he had left that part of the mystery to take care of itself, trusting to his mother-in-law's departure to relieve the situation. No doubt she would have told him the truth herself rather than leave her daughter to the mercy of the men who knew her secret.

But he was still far from suspecting the worst of the truth.

There were a number of men in fancy dominoes; he and Spaulding crossed the lawn in front of the house unchallenged and, passing under the frowning archway, entered the first of the courts.

The oblong sunken pool was banked with myrtle, and above, as well as in the great inner court with the fountain, there were narrow arcaded windows with fluttering silken curtains. Mrs. Thornton had too satiric a sense of humor to have had the famous arabesques of the Alhambra reproduced any more than the massive coats-of-arms above the arches, but the walls were delicately colored, the delicate columns looked like old ivory, and the greatest of the local architects had been entirely successful in combining the massiveness of the warrior stronghold with the airy lightness and spaciousness of the pleasure house.

The bedrooms, Ruyler told Spaulding, were all as modern as they were luxurious, and the library, living-rooms, and dining-room, were in the best American style. Fordy had rebelled at too much "Spanish atmosphere," his blood being straight Anglo-Saxon, and Mrs. Thornton always knew when to yield. Nevertheless, Flora Thornton had built the proper setting for her barbaric beauty, and, possibly, spirit.

People were sitting about the courts on piles of colored silken cushions, those that had got themselves up in Eastern costumes having drifted naturally to the suitable surroundings; for, after all, the Moors had been Mohammedans.

"Don't let's hang round here," said the detective, "and don't stand holding yourself like a ramrod--like that gent out there with the ruff that must be taking the skin off his chin. I kinder thought I'd like to see the whole show, but we'd best go now and wait for our little turn."

He led the way round the building to the rear of the southwest tower. There was a little grove of jasmine trees just beneath it, that made the air overpoweringly sweet, but there were no lights on this side, as the garages, stables, vegetable gardens, and servants' quarters would have destroyed the picture.

Spaulding glanced about sharply, but there was not even a strolling couple, and even the moon was shining on the other side of the heavy mass of buildings.

"Now, listen," he said. "You see this window?"--he indicated one directly over their heads. "At exactly one o'clock, when everybody is flocking to the supper tables on the terraces, I expect some one to lean out of that window and talk to some one who will be waiting just below. There may be no talk, but I think there will be, and I want you to listen to every word of it without so much as drawing a long breath, no matter what is said, until I grab your elbow--like this--then I want you to put up your hand in a hurry while I'm also attendin' to business.

"That's all I'll say now. But by the time a few words have been said, later, I guess you'll be on.

"Now, we must resign ourselves to a long wait without a smoke and to keeping perfectly still. I dared not risk comin' any later for fear the others might be beforehand, too."

Ruyler ground his teeth. He felt ridiculous and humiliated. It was no compensation that he was holding up the wall of a stucco Moorish palace and that some three hundred masked people in fancy dress were within earshot... or did the way he was togged out make him feel all the more absurd? The whole thing was beastly un-American....

But, was it, after all? If he and Helene had been here together to-night, not married and harrowed, but engaged and quick with romance, would he have thought it absurd to conspire and maneuver to separate her from the crowd and snatch a few moments of heavenly solitude? Would he have despised himself for suffering torments if she flouted him or for wanting to murder any man who balked him?

Love, and all the passions, creative and destructive, it engendered, all the sentiments and follies and crimes, to say nothing of ambition and greed and the lust to kill in war--these were instincts and traits that appeared in mankind generation after generation, in every corner civilized and savage of the globe. The world changed somewhat in form during its progress, but never in substance.

And mystery and intrigue were equally a part of life, as indigenous to the Twentieth Century as to those days long entombed in history when the troops of Ferdinand and Isabella sat down on the plain before Grenada.

Plot and melodrama were in every life; in some so briefly as hardly to be recognized, in others--in that of certain men and women in the public eye, for instance--they were almost in the nature of a continuous performance.

In these days men took a bath morning and evening, ate daintily, had a refined vocabulary to use on demand, dressed in tweeds instead of velvet. There were longer intervals between the old style of warfare when men were always plugging one another full of holes in the name of religion or disputed territory, merely to amuse themselves with a tryout of Right against Might, or to gratify the insane ambition of some upstart like Napoleon. To-day the business world was the battlefield, and it was his capital a man was always healing, his poor brain that collapsed nightly after the strain and nervous worry of the day.

It suddenly felt quite normal to be here flattened against a wall waiting for some impossible denouement.

Nevertheless, he was sick with apprehension.

Would it merely be the prelude to another drama? Was his life to be a series of unwritten plays, of which he was both the hero and the bewildered spectator? Or would it bring him calm, the terrible calm of stagnation, of an inner life finished, sealed, buried?

It was inevitable in these romantic surroundings and conditions that he should revert to his almost forgotten jealousy. Suppose Spaulding had stumbled upon something.... But he had been asked for no such evidence.... It would be a damnable liberty.... It might be inextricably woven with the business in hand.... There were other men besides Doremus whom Helene saw constantly.... Spaulding may have seen his chance to nip the thing in the bud, and had taken the risk....

He felt the detective's lips at his ear: "Hear anything? Move a little so's you can look up."

Ruyler heard his wife's voice above him, then Aileen Lawton's. He parted the branches and saw the two girls lean over the low sill of the casement. Both had removed their masks, but their faces were only dimly revealed. Their voices, however, were distinct enough, and his wife's was dull and flat.

"Oh, I can't," she said. "I can't."

"Well, you'll just jolly well have to. You've got it, haven't you?"

"Oh, yes, I've got it!"

"Well, he'll never suspect you."

"I shall tell him."

"Tell him? You little fool. And give us all away?"

"I'd mention no other names."

"As if he wouldn't probe until he found out. Don't you know Price Ruyler yet? My father said once he'd have made a great District Attorney. What's the use of telling him later, for that matter? Why not now?"

"I haven't the courage yet. I might have one day--at just the right moment. I never thought I was a coward."

"You're just a kid. That's what's the matter. We ought to have left you out. I told Polly that--"

"You couldn't! Oh, don't you see you couldn't. That's the terrible part of it! Left me out? I'd have found my way in."

"I'm not so sure. You were interested in heaps of things, and in love, and all that--"

"Oh, I'd like to excuse myself by blaming it on being bored, and tired of trying to amuse myself doing nothing worth while, but it's bad blood, that's what it is, bad blood, and you know it, if none of the others do."

"Oh, I'm not one of your heredity fiends. When did your mother tell you?"

"Only the other day."

"Well, she ought to have told you long ago. I believe you'd have kept out if you'd known."

"Wouldn't I? But of course she hated to tell the truth to me--"

"Well, if I'd known that you didn't know I'd have told you, all right. I wormed it out of Dad soon after you arrived, and at first I thought it was a good joke on Society, to say nothing of Price Ruyler, with his air of God having created heaven first, maybe, but New York just after. Then I got fond of you and I wouldn't have told for the world. But I would have put you on your guard if I'd known."

"Oh, it doesn't matter. Even if Price doesn't find out about this, if he learns the other--who my father was, and that awful men have recognized my mother--I suppose he'll hate me, and in time I'll go back to Rouen--"

"Now, you don't think as ill as that of him, do you? He makes me so mad sometimes I could spit in his face, but if he's one thing he's true blue. He's the straight masculine type with a streak of old romance that would make him love a woman the more, the sorrier he was for her, and the weaker she was--I mean so long as she was young. After this, just get to work on your character, kid. When you're thirty maybe he won't feel that it's his whole duty to protect you. You'll never be hard and seasoned like me, nor able to take care of yourself. I like danger, and excitement, and uncertainty, and mystery, and intrigue, and lying, and wriggling out of tight places. I'd have gone mad in this hole long ago, if I hadn't, for I don't care for sport. But you were intended to develop into what is called a 'fine woman,' surrounded by the right sort of man meanwhile. And Price Ruyler is the right sort. I'll say that much for him. He'd have driven me to drink, but he's just your sort--"

"And what am I doing? I am the most degraded woman in the world."

"Oh, no, you're not. Not by a long sight. You don't know how much worse you could be. One woman who is here to-night I saw lying dead drunk in the road between San Mateo and Burlingame the other day when I was driving with Alice Thorndyke, and Alice is having her fourth or fifth lover, I forget which--"

"They are no worse than I."

"Listen. He's coming. Got it ready?"

"I can't."

"You must. He'll hound you in the *Merry Tattler* until the whole town knows you're a welcher, and not a soul would speak to you. That is the one unpardonable sin--"

"I wish I'd told Price--"

"Oh, no, you don't. This is just a lovely way out. Glad he had the inspiration. Hello, Nick."

A man had groped his way between the trees and stood just under the window.

"What are you doing here?" asked Doremus sourly.

"Witness, witness, my dear Nick. Besides, poor Helene never would have come alone, so there you are."

"To hell with all this melodramatic business. It could have been done anywhere--"

"Not much. Dark corners for dark doings."

"Well, hand it over."

Ruyler had given his brain an icy shower bath as soon as he heard his wife's voice, and was now as cool and alert as even the detective could have wished. He did not wait for the promised impulse to his elbow; his hand shot up just ahead of Doremus's and closed over his wife's hand, which, he felt at once, held the ruby. At the same moment Spaulding caught Doremus by his medieval collar and shook him until the man's teeth chattered, then he slapped his face and kicked him.

"Now, you," he said standing over the panting man, who was mopping his bleeding nose, and holding the electric torch so that it would shine on his own face. "You get out of California, d'you hear? You're a gambler and a blackmailer and a panderer to old women, and I've got some evidence that would drag you into court however it turned out, so's you'd find this town a live gridiron. So, git, while you can. Go while the going's good."

Doremus, too shaken to reply, slunk off, and Spaulding after a glance upward, left as silently.

CHAPTER XIII

I

Aileen had shrieked and fled. Ruyler stood in the room with the ruby in his open hand. He saw that Helene was standing quite erect before him. She had made no attempt to leave the room, nor did she appear to be threatened with hysterics.

He groped until he found the electric button. The room, as Ruyler had inferred, was Mrs. Thornton's winter boudoir, a gorgeous room of yellow brocade and oriental stuffs.

"Will you sit down?" he asked.

Helene shook her head. She was very white and she looked as old as a young actress who has been doing one night stands for three months. Behind the drawn mask of her face there was her indestructible youth, but so faint that it thought itself dead.

She looked at her hands, which she twisted together as if they were cold.

"Will you tell me the truth now?" asked Price.

"Don't you guess it?"

"When I came here to-night I believed that you were the victim of blackmail. I was not watching you--I hope you will take my word for that. We--I had a detective on the case--Spaulding merely wanted to nab the man who was blackmailing you--"

"Do you still believe that?"

"I overheard your conversation with Aileen Lawton. I don't know what to believe."

"I am a gambler. My father was a gambler. He kept a notorious place in San Francisco. His name out here was James Garnett. My grandfather was a gambler. He was even more spectacular--"

"I know all that. Don't mind."

"You knew it?" For the first time she looked at him, but she turned her eyes away at once and stared at the oblong of dark framed by the window. "Why--"

"Spaulding told me to-night only."

"Mother told me a week or so ago. She'd been recognized. Shortly after I married, when she found out how the women played bridge and poker here, she made me promise I'd never touch a card, never play any sort of gambling game. I promised readily enough, and I thought nothing of her insistence. Maman was old-fashioned in many ways--I mean the life we lived in. Rouen was so different from this that I could understand how many things would shock her. I never thought about it--but--it was about six months ago--you were away for a week and I stayed with Polly Roberts at the Fairmont. I knew of course that she played and that Aileen and a lot of the others did, but I hadn't given the matter a thought. One heard nothing but bridge, bridge, bridge. I was sick of the word.

"But I found they played poker. Polly and Aileen, Alice Thorndyke, Janet Maynard, Mary Kimball, Nick Doremus, Rex and one or two other men who could get off in the afternoons.

"I never had dreamed any one in society played for such high stakes. Janet Maynard and Mary Kimball could afford it, but Polly and Alice and Aileen couldn't. Still they often won--enough, anyhow, to clean up and go on. Doremus is a wonderful player. That is how I got interested, watching him after he had explained the game to me.

"It was a long time before I was persuaded to take a hand. It was so interesting just to watch. And not only the game, but their faces. Some would have a regular 'poker face,' others would give themselves away. Once Aileen had the most awful hysterics. We were afraid some one outside would hear her; the deadening was burnt out of the walls of the Fairmont at the time of the fire. But we were in the middle room of the suite.

"Nick told her in his dreadful cold expressionless voice that if she ever did that again he'd never play another game with her. That meant that they'd all drop her, and she came to and promised, and she kept her word. Poker is the breath of life to her. I think she'd become a drug fiend if she couldn't have it.

"At last they persuaded me to play. We were playing at Nick's, and after a light dinner served by his Jap, we went right on playing until midnight. I never thought of you or anything. I seemed to respond with every nerve in my body and brain. I won and won and won, and even when I lost I didn't mind. The sensation, the tearing excitement just under a perfectly cool brain was wonderful.

"I only ceased to enjoy it when I realized what it meant. When I couldn't keep away from it. When I lived for the hour when we would meet,--at Polly's, or at Nick's or at Aileen's--any of the places where we were supposed to be dancing, but where there was no danger of being found out. Of course I dared not have them at home, and the others lived with their families, or had too many servants....

"I came fully to my senses one day when Nick told me I was a born gambler if ever there was one. Then, when I realized, I became desperately unhappy.

"I was the slave of a thing. I was deceiving you. When I was at the table I loved poker better than you, better than anything on earth. When I was alone I hated it. But I couldn't break away. Besides, I didn't always win. I had to play in the hope of winning back. Or if I won a lot it was a point of honor to go on and play again, and give them their chance.

"Mrs. Thornton found out. She gave me a terrible talking to. I am afraid I was very insolent.

"But she came up that night of the Assembly and warned me that you were down stairs. I was playing in Polly's room. We had all danced two or three times and then slipped up to the next floor by different stairs and lifts. I liked her better then. Of course she did it for your sake, not mine. But she's a good sort, not a cat.

"You have not noticed, but I have not bought a new gown this season except that little gray one and this--which was made in the house. I dared not pawn my jewels, for fear you would miss them.

"I have been in hell.

"Then--it was that evening you heard maman reproach me for breaking my promise--I had lost a dreadful lot of money and Nick had scurried round and borrowed it for me. I didn't know then that he meant all the time to get hold of the ruby--I am sure now that he cheated and made me lose.

"Well, I sent the maid away that night and told maman. She was nearly off her head. I never saw her excited before. Then she told me the truth. I felt as if I had been turned to stone. But I felt suddenly cool and wary. I knew I must keep my head. It was as if my father had suddenly come alive in my brain. I had never lied to you before, merely put you off. But how I lied that night! I felt possessed. But I knew I must not be found out, and I made up my mind to stop playing as soon as I came out even. If I had known that my father and my grandfather had been gamblers I never should have touched a card. I'd far rather have drunk poison.

"I made up my mind then, and there to stop and I felt quite capable of it. But I had to go on and square myself, for I owed that money to Nick. But when I played it was with my head only. All the fever had gone out of my veins. I loathed it. I loathed still more deceiving you.

"I won and won and won. I thought I was delivered. I was almost happy again. Some day I meant to tell you--when it was all over.

"Then I began to lose horribly. Thousands. It ran up to twenty thousand. I did not betray myself, and the girls thought I had money of my own and could pay my losses quite easily. They didn't know that Nick always helped me out. He was never the least bit in love with me--he couldn't love any woman--but he said I played such a wonderful game and was such a sport, never lost my head, that he wouldn't lose me for the world--when I threatened to stop and never play again.

"But all the time he wanted the ruby. I found that out when he told me he must have the money inside of a week; he'd taken it out of his business, and it really belonged to his partners, and they'd find him out and send him to prison--

"I offered him my jewels. They would have brought half their value at least. I could have told you they were stolen--only one more lie. It was then he said he must have the ruby. He had known about it ever since you came out here, but after he saw it on me that night at the Gwynnes' he was more than ever determined to have it.

"I laughed at him at first. It seemed preposterous that he could demand a ruby worth two or three hundred thousand dollars in payment for a debt of twenty thousand. I thought of selling my jewels and furs and laces, or pawning them and raising the amount--he only had my I.O.U. for that sum. But I didn't know where to go. So I told Aileen. She wouldn't hear of my disposing of my things, said it would, be all over town in twenty-four hours. She advised me to get the twenty thousand out of you on one pretext or another.

"I tried. You will remember. Then Nick began to haunt me. He whispered in my ear wherever we met. I was nearly frantic. He said he could hold me up to shame without compromising himself. I had written him some frantic letters, and he said they read just like--like--the other thing.

"I felt perfectly helpless. I knew that even if I did manage to pawn the jewels, you would miss them from the safe and trace them. I ceased to feel cool. I nearly went off my head. But I stopped gambling. I felt sure by this time that he could make me lose, but I couldn't prove it. Aileen told me I must give him the ruby. He promised me before Aileen that he would give me back my I.O.U.'s as well as my notes if I would hand over the ruby. He knew I was to wear it to-night.

"Finally I gave in. Yesterday Nick called me up on the telephone and told me to come down to the California Market to lunch, and to bring Aileen. He told me there that unless I promised to give him the ruby to-night, and kept my word, he'd either give my I.O.U.'s and my notes to you or to the *Merry Tattler*. He didn't care which. I could have my choice.

"I said I would do it. But it was terribly conspicuous. Everybody would notice when it was gone. He said I must conceal it anyhow until we unmasked after supper, and then I could pretend I had lost it. He discussed several plans for having me slip it to him, but it was Aileen who insisted we should come here. Mrs. Thornton never opens her boudoir at a party. Everywhere else would be a blaze of light. In this dark corner we should be safe, especially if he came from the outside and I from inside. How did your detective find out?"

"I think Aileen did a decent thing for once in her life."

She went on in her monotonous voice. "I felt reckless after that and I really was gay and almost happy at dinner last night. The die was cast. I didn't much care for anything. I thought perhaps it was my last night with you--that when I told you I had lost the ruby you would suspect and turn me out of your house, tell maman to take me back to Rouen.

"Then came that awful moment when you said you had to go away and I could not wear it. For a few moments I thought I should scream and tell you everything. But I was both too proud and too much of a coward. Then I knew I should have to rob the safe, and somehow I hated that part more than anything else. I did it just ten minutes before Rex and Polly called for me to motor down here. It had seemed the most horrible thing in the world to be a gambler, but it was worse to be a thief.

"I remembered the combination perfectly. I have that sort of memory: it registers photographically. I had seen you move the combination several times. Perhaps I deliberately registered it. I can't say. I have lived in such a maze of intrigue lately. I can't say. That is all--except that I didn't get the letters and the other things."

"He had an envelope in one hand. Spaulding has it beyond a doubt."

CHAPTER XIV

There was silence for a moment and then Price said awkwardly: "It is a pity you haven't the chain or you could wear the ruby for the rest of the evening."

She turned her eyes from the window and stared at him. "I have the chain--" She raised her hand to the tip of her bodice--"but--but--you can't mean--it isn't possible that you can forgive me."

"I think I have taken very bad care of you. What are you, after all, but a brilliant child? I am thirty-three--"

He suddenly tore off his domino with, a feeling of rage, and thrust his hands into his friendly pockets. He had never made many verbal protestations to her, although the most exacting wife could have found no fault with his love-making. But to-night he felt dumb; he was mortally afraid of appearing high and noble and magnanimous.

"You see, things always happen during the first years of married life. Perhaps more happens--I mean in a pettier way--when the man has leisure and can see too much of his wife. In my case--our case--it was the other way--and something almost tragic happened. So I vote we treat it casually, as something that must have been expected sooner or later to disturb our--our--even tenor--and forget it."

"Forget it?"

"Well, yes. I can if you can."

"And can you forget who I am?"

"You are exactly what you were before those scoundrels recognized your mother, and--and--set me going. Of course I had to find out the truth. I thought you knew and tried to make you tell me. But you wouldn't--couldn't--and I had to employ Spaulding."

"Do you mean you would have married me if you had known the truth at the time?"

"Rather."

"And--but--I told you--I became a regular gambler."

He could not help smiling. "I have no fear of your gambling again. And I don't fancy you were a bit worse than the others who had no gambling blood in them--all the world has that. Gambling is about the earliest of the vices. I--if--you wouldn't mind promising--I know you will keep it."

"Nothing under heaven would induce me to play again. But--but--I opened your safe like a thief and stole--"

"Oh, not quite. After all it was yours as much as mine. If I had died without a will you would have got it.

"Of course--I know what you mean--but men have always driven women into a corner, and they have had to get out by methods of their own. I wish now I had given you the twenty thousand. I prefer you should accept my decision that it was all my fault. Give me the chain."

She drew it from her bosom and handed it to him. He fastened the ruby in its place and threw the chain over her neck. The great jewel lit up the front of her somber gown like a sudden torch in a cavern.

The stern despair of Helene's tragic mask relaxed. She dropped her face into her hands and began to sob. Then Ruyler was himself again. He picked her up in his arms and settled comfortably into the deepest of the chairs.

The Codes Of Hammurabi And Moses
W. W. Davies

QTY

The discovery of the Hammurabi Code is one of the greatest achievements of archaeology, and is of paramount interest, not only to the student of the Bible, but also to all those interested in ancient history...

Religion   **ISBN:** *1-59462-338-4*   **Pages:132**
MSRP $12.95

The Theory of Moral Sentiments
Adam Smith

QTY

This work from 1749. contains original theories of conscience amd moral judgment and it is the foundation for systemof morals.

Philosophy   **ISBN:** *1-59462-777-0*   **Pages:536**
MSRP $19.95

Jessica's First Prayer
Hesba Stretton

QTY

In a screened and secluded corner of one of the many railway-bridges which span the streets of London there could be seen a few years ago, from five o'clock every morning until half past eight, a tidily set-out coffee-stall, consisting of a trestle and board, upon which stood two large tin cans, with a small fire of charcoal burning under each so as to keep the coffee boiling during the early hours of the morning when the work-people were thronging into the city on their way to their daily toil...

Pages:84

Childrens   **ISBN:** *1-59462-373-2*   *MSRP $9.95*

My Life and Work
Henry Ford

QTY

Henry Ford revolutionized the world with his implementation of mass production for the Model T automobile. Gain valuable business insight into his life and work with his own auto-biography... "We have only started on our development of our country we have not as yet, with all our talk of wonderful progress, done more than scratch the surface. The progress has been wonderful enough but..."

Pages:300

Biographies/   **ISBN:** *1-59462-198-5*   *MSRP $21.95*

The Art of Cross-Examination
Francis Wellman

QTY

I presume it is the experience of every author, after his first book is published upon an important subject, to be almost overwhelmed with a wealth of ideas and illustrations which could readily have been included in his book, and which to his own mind, at least, seem to make a second edition inevitable. Such certainly was the case with me; and when the first edition had reached its sixth impression in five months, I rejoiced to learn that it seemed to my publishers that the book had met with a sufficiently favorable reception to justify a second and considerably enlarged edition. ..

Reference   ISBN: *1-59462-647-2*

Pages:412

MSRP $19.95

On the Duty of Civil Disobedience
Henry David Thoreau

QTY

Thoreau wrote his famous essay, On the Duty of Civil Disobedience, as a protest against an unjust but popular war and the immoral but popular institution of slave-owning. He did more than write—he declined to pay his taxes, and was hauled off to gaol in consequence. Who can say how much this refusal of his hastened the end of the war and of slavery ?

Law   ISBN: *1-59462-747-9*

Pages:48

MSRP $7.45

Dream Psychology Psychoanalysis for Beginners
Sigmund Freud

QTY

Sigmund Freud, born Sigismund Schlomo Freud (May 6, 1856 - September 23, 1939), was a Jewish-Austrian neurologist and psychiatrist who co-founded the psychoanalytic school of psychology. Freud is best known for his theories of the unconscious mind, especially involving the mechanism of repression; his redefinition of sexual desire as mobile and directed towards a wide variety of objects; and his therapeutic techniques, especially his understanding of transference in the therapeutic relationship and the presumed value of dreams as sources of insight into unconscious desires.

Psychology   ISBN: *1-59462-905-6*

Pages:196

MSRP $15.45

The Miracle of Right Thought
Orison Swett Marden

QTY

Believe with all of your heart that you will do what you were made to do. When the mind has once formed the habit of holding cheerful, happy, prosperous pictures, it will not be easy to form the opposite habit. It does not matter how improbable or how far away this realization may see, or how dark the prospects may be, if we visualize them as best we can, as vividly as possible, hold tenaciously to them and vigorously struggle to attain them, they will gradually become actualized, realized in the life. But a desire, a longing without endeavor, a yearning abandoned or held indifferently will vanish without realization.

Self Help   ISBN: *1-59462-644-8*

Pages:360

MSRP $25.45

QTY

The Rosicrucian Cosmo-Conception Mystic Christianity *by Max Heindel*   ISBN: *1-59462-188-8*   **$38.95**
The Rosicrucian Cosmo-conception is not dogmatic, neither does it appeal to any other authority than the reason of the student. It is: not controversial, but is: sent forth in the, hope that it may help to clear...   New Age/Religion Pages 646

Abandonment To Divine Providence *by Jean-Pierre de Caussade*   ISBN: *1-59462-228-0*   **$25.95**
"The Rev. Jean Pierre de Caussade was one of the most remarkable spiritual writers of the Society of Jesus in France in the 18th Century. His death took place at Toulouse in 1751. His works have gone through many editions and have been republished...   Inspirational/Religion Pages 400

Mental Chemistry *by Charles Haanel*   ISBN: *1-59462-192-6*   **$23.95**
Mental Chemistry allows the change of material conditions by combining and appropriately utilizing the power of the mind. Much like applied chemistry creates something new and unique out of careful combinations of chemicals the mastery of mental chemistry...   New Age Pages 354

The Letters of Robert Browning and Elizabeth Barret Barrett 1845-1846 vol II   ISBN: *1-59462-193-4*   **$35.95**
by Robert Browning and Elizabeth Barrett   Biographies Pages 596

Gleanings In Genesis (volume I) *by Arthur W. Pink*   ISBN: *1-59462-130-6*   **$27.45**
Appropriately has Genesis been termed "the seed plot of the Bible" for in it we have, in germ form, almost all of the great doctrines which are afterwards fully developed in the books of Scripture which follow...   Religion/Inspirational Pages 420

The Master Key *by L. W. de Laurence*   ISBN: *1-59462-001-6*   **$30.95**
In no branch of human knowledge has there been a more lively increase of the spirit of research during the past few years than in the study of Psychology, Concentration and Mental Discipline. The requests for authentic lessons in Thought Control, Mental Discipline and...   New Age/Business Pages 422

The Lesser Key Of Solomon Goetia *by L. W. de Laurence*   ISBN: *1-59462-092-X*   **$9.95**
This translation of the first book of the "Lernegton" which is now for the first time made accessible to students of Talismanic Magic was done, after careful collation and edition, from numerous Ancient Manuscripts in Hebrew, Latin, and French...   New Age/Occult Pages 92

Rubaiyat Of Omar Khayyam *by Edward Fitzgerald*   ISBN:*1-59462-332-5*   **$13.95**
Edward Fitzgerald, whom the world has already learned, in spite of his own efforts to remain within the shadow of anonymity, to look upon as one of the rarest poets of the century, was born at Bredfield, in Suffolk, on the 31st of March, 1809. He was the third son of John Purcell...   Music Pages 172

Ancient Law *by Henry Maine*   ISBN: *1-59462-128-4*   **$29.95**
The chief object of the following pages is to indicate some of the earliest ideas of mankind, as they are reflected in Ancient Law, and to point out the relation of those ideas to modern thought.   Religiom/History Pages 452

Far-Away Stories *by William J. Locke*   ISBN: *1-59462-129-2*   **$19.45**
"Good wine needs no bush, but a collection of mixed vintages does. And this book is just such a collection. Some of the stories I do not want to remain buried for ever in the museum files of dead magazine-numbers an author's not unpardonable vanity..."   Fiction Pages 272

Life of David Crockett *by David Crockett*   ISBN: *1-59462-250-7*   **$27.45**
"Colonel David Crockett was one of the most remarkable men of the times in which he lived. Born in humble life, but gifted with a strong will, an indomitable courage, and unremitting perseverance...   Biographies/New Age Pages 424

Lip-Reading *by Edward Nitchie*   ISBN: *1-59462-206-X*   **$25.95**
Edward B. Nitchie, founder of the New York School for the Hard of Hearing, now the Nitchie School of Lip-Reading, Inc, wrote "LIP-READING Principles and Practice". The development and perfecting of this meritorious work on lip-reading was an undertaking...   How-to Pages 400

A Handbook of Suggestive Therapeutics, Applied Hypnotism, Psychic Science   ISBN: *1-59462-214-0*   **$24.95**
by Henry Munro   Health/New Age/Health/Self-help Pages 376

A Doll's House: and Two Other Plays *by Henrik Ibsen*   ISBN: *1-59462-112-8*   **$19.95**
Henrik Ibsen created this classic when in revolutionary 1848 Rome. Introducing some striking concepts in playwriting for the realist genre, this play has been studied the world over.   Fiction/Classics/Plays 308

The Light of Asia *by sir Edwin Arnold*   ISBN: *1-59462-204-3*   **$13.95**
In this poetic masterpiece, Edwin Arnold describes the life and teachings of Buddha. The man who was to become known as Buddha to the world was born as Prince Gautama of India but he rejected the worldly riches and abandoned the reigns of power when...   Religion/History/Biographies Pages 170

The Complete Works of Guy de Maupassant *by Guy de Maupassant*   ISBN: *1-59462-157-8*   **$16.95**
"For days and days, nights and nights, I had dreamed of that first kiss which was to consecrate our engagement, and I knew not on what spot I should put my lips..."   Fiction/Classics Pages 240

The Art of Cross-Examination *by Francis L. Wellman*   ISBN: *1-59462-309-0*   **$26.95**
Written by a renowned trial lawyer, Wellman imparts his experience and uses case studies to explain how to use psychology to extract desired information through questioning.   How-to/Science/Reference Pages 408

Answered or Unanswered? *by Louisa Vaughan*   ISBN: *1-59462-248-5*   **$10.95**
Miracles of Faith in China   Religion Pages 112

The Edinburgh Lectures on Mental Science (1909) *by Thomas*   ISBN: *1-59462-008-3*   **$11.95**
This book contains the substance of a course of lectures recently given by the writer in the Queen Street Hail, Edinburgh. Its purpose is to indicate the Natural Principles governing the relation between Mental Action and Material Conditions...   New Age/Psychology Pages 148

Ayesha *by H. Rider Haggard*   ISBN: *1-59462-301-5*   **$24.95**
Verily and indeed it is the unexpected that happens! Probably if there was one person upon the earth from whom the Editor of this, and of a certain previous history, did not expect to hear again...   Classics Pages 380

Ayala's Angel *by Anthony Trollope*   ISBN: *1-59462-352-X*   **$29.95**
The two girls were both pretty, but Lucy who was twenty-one who supposed to be simple and comparatively unattractive, whereas Ayala was credited, as her Bombwhat romantic name might show, with poetic charm and a taste for romance. Ayala when her father died was nineteen...   Fiction Pages 484

The American Commonwealth *by James Bryce*   ISBN: *1-59462-286-8*   **$34.45**
An interpretation of American democratic political theory. It examines political mechanics and society from the perspective of Scotsman James Bryce   Politics Pages 572

Stories of the Pilgrims *by Margaret P. Pumphrey*   ISBN: *1-59462-116-0*   **$17.95**
This book explores pilgrims religious oppression in England as well as their escape to Holland and eventual crossing to America on the Mayflower, and their early days in New England...   History Pages 268

QTY

The Fasting Cure *by Sinclair Upton*   ISBN: *1-59462-222-1* **$13.95**
In the Cosmopolitan Magazine for May, 1910, and in the Contemporary Review (London) for April, 1910, I published an article dealing with my experiences in fasting. I have written a great many magazine articles, but never one which attracted so much attention... New Age/Self Help/Health Pages 164

Hebrew Astrology *by Sepharial*   ISBN: *1-59462-308-2* **$13.45**
In these days of advanced thinking it is a matter of common observation that we have left many of the old landmarks behind and that we are now pressing forward to greater heights and to a wider horizon than that which represented the mind-content of our progenitors... Astrology Pages 144

Thought Vibration or The Law of Attraction in the Thought World   ISBN: *1-59462-127-6* **$12.95**
by William Walker Atkinson   Psychology/Religion Pages 144

Optimism *by Helen Keller*   ISBN: *1-59462-108-X* **$15.95**
Helen Keller was blind, deaf, and mute since 19 months old, yet famously learned how to overcome these handicaps, communicate with the world, and spread her lectures promoting optimism. An inspiring read for everyone... Biographies/Inspirational Pages 84

Sara Crewe *by Frances Burnett*   ISBN: *1-59462-360-0* **$9.45**
In the first place, Miss Minchin lived in London. Her home was a large, dull, tall one, in a large, dull square, where all the houses were alike, and all the sparrows were alike, and where all the door-knockers made the same heavy sound... Childrens/Classic Pages 88

The Autobiography of Benjamin Franklin *by Benjamin Franklin*   ISBN: *1-59462-135-7* **$24.95**
The Autobiography of Benjamin Franklin has probably been more extensively read than any other American historical work, and no other book of its kind has had such ups and downs of fortune. Franklin lived for many years in England, where he was agent... Biographies/History Pages 332

Name	
Email	
Telephone	
Address	
City, State ZIP	

☐ **Credit Card**   ☐ **Check / Money Order**

Credit Card Number	
Expiration Date	
Signature	

Please Mail to: Book Jungle
                    PO Box 2226
                    Champaign, IL 61825
or Fax to: 630-214-0564

ORDERING INFORMATION

web*: www.bookjungle.com*
email*: sales@bookjungle.com*
fax*: 630-214-0564*
mail*: Book Jungle PO Box 2226 Champaign, IL 61825*
or PayPal *to sales@bookjungle.com*

Please contact us for bulk discounts

DIRECT-ORDER TERMS

**20% Discount if You Order
Two or More Books**
Free Domestic Shipping!
Accepted: Master Card, Visa,
Discover, American Express